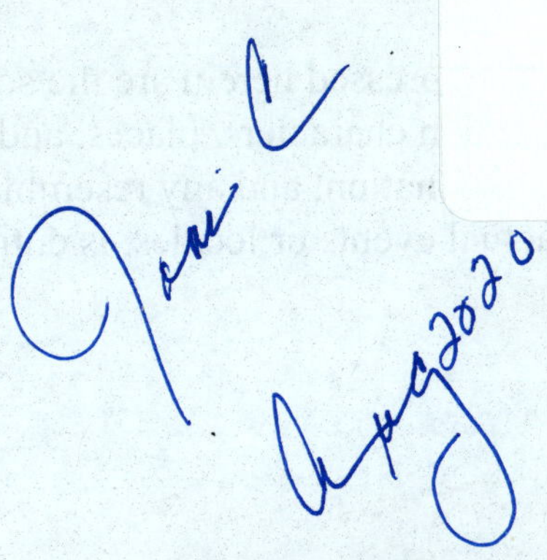

At Witt's End

By J.V. Caggiano

This is a work of fiction, and the views expressed herein are the sole responsibility of the author. Likewise, certain characters, places, and incidents are the product of the author's imagination, and any resemblance to actual persons, living or dead, or actual events or locales, is entirely coincidental.

At Witt's End

Published 2020

Printed in the United States of America

ISBN: 978-0-578-64596-4

Chapter 1

Cerridwen drummed her fingers on the desk in frustration. It had been four solid hours and still she had not broken Hal Norland. She knew he had killed his wife. She had been there when he did it. She watched his rage build, seen his temper unravel and then fray. She had witnessed each stroke of the knife, each blow. His guilt was proven fact. But she still didn't know why.

She rubbed her eyes and then tried to bore a hole in the computer screen with her stare. The results were negligible at best. Hal Fucking Norland. Cerridwen was coming to hate that fictional bastard. Hadn't she created him, breathed life into his twisted little soul? And after 275 pages this was how the snake repaid her! He was going to ruin her damn book. For two cents and a chocolate bar she would hit delete and put an end to him. But with a deadline looming, it was not an option, and the little deviant knew it, too.

The phone shrilled. Without turning her eyes from the blinking cursor, she grabbed the handset and absently pressed talk and end in quick succession. She needed that dénouement. There was no ending without it. When you waded through nearly 300 pages, you wanted to know why. The puzzle was part of the game, but most readers wanted to know why. She chewed her lip in thought.

The doorbell rang and Cerridwen ignored it. There was always the nut job option, she mused. No, really that was the easy way out.

The phone started to ring again. She silenced it for the second time without looking at it. It was kind of a cop out. *Oh, he did it 'cause he was crazy, don't you know?*

The doorbell sounded again. She responded with a rude gesture in the vague direction of the front door. Back to the book. Besides, there was enough of that unimaginative crap in real life...fiction was creative.

The phone and the doorbell were now singing in concert. Rolling her chair slightly to the left she reached down and yanked the phone cord out of the jack. The damn doorbell persisted in solo. With a string of curses blue enough to do her Daddy proud, she kicked out of her chair and stomped barefoot towards the front of the house. Whoever was ringing the door bell was lucky she had bothered to get dressed. Didn't anybody understand she was working?

"Oh, you're home. So even though you work from home, you can't be busy. After all, it's not like you're, you know, working or anything," she mumbled under her breath. As she passed through the kitchen she paused momentarily, distracted by the knife block. She yanked out the ten inch chef's knife that might just be the solution to her plot difficulties.

The doorbell shrilled again. "If it's that bitch from the Historical Society I swear to God I'm going to kill her and bury her in the backyard. And then I'm putting a sign on the door saying we have the plague." In the year since she had inherited her grandmother's house there had been a visit from the Historical Society at least once a week.

She wrenched the door open, ready to blister Miss Hawkner's ears, only to find a stranger. The clean cut, button down man seemed taken aback by her sudden appearance. Her bare feet seemed to give him pause, but evidently the pedicure was reassuring. His eyes traveled up her dark jeans to her black cashmere sweater as she tapped her toes impatiently. By the time he reached well cared for hair and expertly applied makeup, he felt himself on solid ground again. Maybe he hadn't noticed the one raised eyebrow.

"Can I help you?" Her voice was icy.

"I can help you!" he asserted, straightening his tie.

"I sincerely doubt it."

"I have here the world's only true miracle cleanser." He thrust the bottle towards her.

She fended it off with the chef's knife. Seriously, who sold anything door to door anymore? On Sunday, for Christ sake! And on top of that, he was using sloppy language. She could not stand people who were sloppy with language. "And what leads you to believe I need my miracles cleansed?"

"What? Oh, I see. No, ha, ha. The cleanser itself is the miracle."

Cerridwen moved to shut the door.

"There is no stain it can't remove. Tomato sauce, ink, oil, even blood!"

Her attention snagged on the last word. Instead of closing the door, she leaned against it and folded her arms. "Blood?"

"Yes, blood. Lifts it right off. Any stain gone in seconds."

"So, Patrick." She peered at his name tag. "How much blood are we talking?"

"Excuse me?" He frowned, confused. He was not prepared to go off script.

"How much blood? Are we talking about a little smear? A 'whoops, I cut myself and now there's these spots all down my favorite shirt' blood? Or can you save my carpet after I forgot to lay a tarp down before I axed my husband to death? Come on, Patrick, give me a ballpark."

Patrick started to back away.

* * * *

Thomas felt the heavy roar of the bus engine in his bones. It was oddly relaxing and made a nice counterpoint to the heavy bass pouring through his headphones. There were next to no passengers early on a Sunday morning, so there was room for him to stretch out. Sometimes it was nice not to be bothered.

"Mr. Rakmelevich?" The thought had conjured one of his favorite students. "Mr. Rakmelevich, is that you?" As if the little monster didn't know it was.

"Yes, Marcos, it's me." Thomas tugged out his ear buds and unfolded himself from the bench seat.

"Marcos, don't talk to strangers," a woman said. "I tell you and I tell you."

"But Mom, it's not a stranger. It's Mr. Rakmelevich, my music teacher."

The tired looking woman with the shopping bags and the strong resemblance to Marcos eyed him cautiously.

He would be the first to admit he was not your stereotypical school music teacher. At six nine and three quarters, with about three feet of black hair down his back, he wasn't the professional standard. But he couldn't help his size, and it was his hair, after all. As far as the ratty jeans and the motorcycle jacket, well, it was his day off. All the same, he faced Mrs. Garcia with trepidation. He was still smarting from the encounter with the PTA president at the Loose Wheel. Sure, it wasn't a place you wanted to find your kid's teacher, but let she who didn't dance on tables throw the first stone. And it was his freaking *day off!*

Mrs. Garcia smiled at him. "Marcos speaks very highly of you. You're his favorite teacher. He talks about nothing but music when he comes home."

Well, that took the wind out of his sails. Actually, it made him feel a little warm and fuzzy.

"Thank you, Mrs. Garcia. It's nice to feel appreciated every once in a while." Thomas felt his face crack in an unfamiliar smile.

"Tell me about it!" She rolled her eyes at Marcos and his younger brother clambering over the seats of the nearly empty bus.

The bus lumbered to a stop. Thomas unfolded from the seat and watched Mrs. Garcia's eyes widen as his head nearly brushed the ceiling. Stepping onto the curb, Thomas cut across the parking lot towards the gas station. It was a tiny, locally owned place that clung to life with the lowest gas prices in town. The attached garage stayed afloat with a string of wealthy clients and their antique cars.

He saw Gerry—roommate, band mate, and mechanic extraordinaire—standing outside the garage with the head mechanic.

They were studying the side of the building where someone had used red spray paint to scrawl "Where Did Mary Go" in three-foot-high letters. The question had appeared all over town in the month he had been living in Victoria, Washington.

"They forgot the question mark," Gerry pointed out helpfully.

"Yeah," sighed the mechanic. "If there is one thing I hate more than graffiti, it's graffiti with bad grammar. And how would I know where Mary went? I don't even know a Mary."

"Publicity stunt?" Thomas offered.

"For what?" Gerry asked

"A punk band maybe." Thomas shrugged. "Pretty good band name, actually," he said over his shoulder as he walked away.

The winding foot path took him around the new condos and a smattering of McMansions—overpriced, under-cooked, and tasteless, but they were not his ultimate destination. Past the park, crowning the hill, was a neighborhood where a hundred years ago they would not have let him clean the toilets. But time and economic downturn come to all, so if you knew a guy whose great uncle was round the bend, three or four of you could afford to live in crumbling gentility that would make a Vanderbilt weep with envy.

Putting his ear buds back in, he started up the hill through the damp Technicolor of a rainy October day. His motorcycle boots slapped the gravel path in time to the drums and heavy bass. The beat carried him along, up the wide sweep of stone steps climbing the hill awash in fall Camellias to the road above. Here the autumn sun had not penetrated the dense trees that lined the avenue. The rising mist from the stream and the lack of light combined to turn this part of his route into a moody metal album cover.

He was distantly aware of voices as he crossed the bridge arcing over the stream. They grew louder as he entered Green Man "Court" which was actually a triangle. The neo-Gothic horror of Gate House was on his right as he entered the court. Farther in that direction were the sweeping lawns of a faux Italian villa. Beyond that was the solid late Victorian groundskeeper's cottage. Veering to the left, he neared Witt's End, the enormous rambling love letter of a house that capped one angle. The front of the house was an organic swirl of white, curving plaster, and flowing marble.

Thomas looked in the gate. The asymmetrical stairs swept down from the small portico and around a small terrace. A man was inching his way down those stairs, his back against the railing, almost sliding down it. The raised voices were coming from him and the woman standing in the doorway. And it was then that Foreigner started to play "Waiting For a Girl Like You" inside his head. It was the knife that did it.

Chapter 2

"Look lady, I just sell the stuff. I don't make it!" Patrick protested, backing away.

"I didn't ask if you made it. I asked you how it worked. Considering you're flogging it on my doorstep, it seems a perfectly reasonable question," Cerridwen pointed out patiently.

Patrick tried a different tact as he searched for an escape route. "Crime scene cleanup is not part of my expertise."

"Well, it seems to me you've neglected a vital area of market research, Patrick."

"I don't do market research!" His voice took on a frantic note as he eyed the knife. "I just sell this stuff!"

The gate creaked and they both turned at the sound.

Cerridwen's first thought was, "Where does he find clothes in that size?" The man's head brushed the Clematis of the arbor as he came up the walk. The seams of his motorcycle jacket creaked in protest as he pushed his hair out of his face. There was a lot of lean muscle there, she noticed, the kind you got from actually using those muscles rather than hours of weightlifting. He came to a stop three steps below them. Cerridwen's eyes were almost level with his. *Christ, just how tall is he?* she thought. It was always the details that caught her.

"Is this guy bothering you?" Somehow it didn't seem like a cliché delivered in a voice that could give the ocean lessons in depth.

"No! No, he is not. He was just leaving!" The ill-fated Patrick explained in the third person as he fled.

"I think, if pressed, he would tell you it was the other way around," Cerridwen told the newcomer. "Whereas I can only say his employers sent him out into the world woefully unprepared."

One enviable eyebrow rose in question. "Unprepared for what?"

"Everything, apparently." Her eyes slid past him to the flash of movement on the street. "Hide!" she hissed.

"From what?" Good question. At that size there probably wasn't much he hid from.

"From Miss Hawkner," she answered him. Forgetting the knife in her hand, she grabbed the front of his jacket and attempted to haul him through the open front door. Predictably, he didn't move an inch. Amused by her effort and unperturbed by the knife waving under his nose, he allowed her to tow him into the house.

She slammed the door, rattling the hundred-year-old stained glass in its frame. "Down," she ordered and he good naturedly allowed himself to be shoved to the floor.

"And who is Miss Hawkner?" he asked conversationally. He watched with interest as she crouched on the floor, peering out the side lights, still clutching the knife.

"That is Miss Hawkner, the vice president of the Historical Society and bane of my existence."

"Interesting word, bane. I knew a guy named Bane once. He wore a lot of eyeliner. Does Miss Hawkner wear a lot of eyeliner?" Her new friend stretched out his legs and prepared to stay awhile.

"Upon occasion. I don't see the relevance."

"Oh, there isn't any. I was just thinking he's the only guy I know with a recording contract. So maybe I should wear eyeliner." He shrugged.

She slid over to sit next to him, their backs against the door. She had to look up to meet his eyes. A brilliant deep green, they were framed by ridiculously long double rows of lashes that any girl would kill for. Set against olive skin, the combination was startling.

"I don't think you need eyeliner," Cerridwen assured him. "What time is it? Is it noon yet?"

"Maybe?" he offered. "Why"

"Time for cake," she answered, gesturing towards the kitchen at the back of the house. "We'll probably have to crawl."

* * * *

Thomas contemplated cake at knife point. Well, not literally. She had stopped waving the knife at him. *What the hell,* he thought. It wasn't as if he had anything better to do. He gauged the distance to the kitchen. It was a pretty big house.

"Do we have to crawl?" he asked. "I mean I'm game, but is it necessary?"

His knife-wielding vision moved to look out the side light again. "I think she's gone the other way. Probably going to hassle poor Felix across the court. We could risk walking to the kitchen," she allowed.

Thomas heaved himself to his feet and offered her a hand up. She led him down the cavernous hall that still managed to be brightly lit. They passed a sweeping marble staircase, with silver-toned metal twisted into branches that gave the impression the railing had grown up the stairs. The tree motif echoed against the white plaster of the adjacent wall. A swinging door led into a kitchen straight out of *Better Homes and Gardens* circa 1922. A wall of windows, broken only by a pair of floor-to-ceiling French doors, flooded the space with light. The room was dominated by a massive marble-topped table, scarred and dull with age but still impressive as all get out. Not knowing what else to do with himself, he pulled out one of the chairs and winced as it creaked under his weight.

His hostess pulled a towering cream and chocolate confection out of a fridge that appeared to have arrived sometime in the 90s. He noticed that she had put down the knife to do this. A pot of tea and some sandwich makings joined the cake on the table. He started to wonder if all of this was for his benefit when there was a knock on the French doors seconds before they burst open in a whirlwind of chiffon. As the scarves settled, the woman at their center eyed Thomas like a car dealer appraising a trade-in.

"Cerridwen, dearest, where did you find this jewel?"

Cerridwen licked chocolate shavings off her fingers before answering. "Morning, Ruby. I found him on the doorstep."

"You had him delivered? Brilliant!" Ruby replied with enthusiasm.

"No. He just sort of showed up." Cerridwen answered offhand, paying more attention the cake than to Thomas.

"Did he? And what is he doing in your kitchen?"

"I offered him cake. At knife point."

"And he accepted. Now why would you do that?" Ruby addressed him directly.

"Because when I look at her I hear 80s power ballads in my head," he answered honestly. Both women studied him with interest.

"Do you often suffer from auditory hallucinations?" Ruby inquired.

"No. I just hear music in my head all the time."

"Isn't that the same thing?"

"No, It isn't." Before he could explain, Ruby decided that introductions were in order.

"I'm Ruby Sands. I used to be a Burlesque Queen. Then I was a Scream Queen 'cause it paid better. Now I'm just a scream."

He laughed as she wiggled her eyebrows suggestively.

"My sister Pearl will be along in a mo. She's banging out a sex scene."

Thomas choked on the tea he'd just swallowed.

Ruby grinned at him. "She writes books, you know."

"No, I didn't know."

"Yes, what my mother used to call pot boilers. I think they call them romances these days. Oh, no sandwiches for me, thanks, dear. Just cake. I have to watch my girlish figure, you know. Yes, she's written something like a million books. Pearl Sands, have you heard of her?"

Thomas shook his head.

"No I don't suppose you read romances, do you?" Before he could answer, she switched subjects with breath taking speed. "What do you do for a living?"

"I teach music to children at a private school."

"Fascinating. Do you play professionally outside of school?"

He didn't have a chance to explain about the band he was trying to get off the ground. Pounding footsteps heralded the arrival of a more spherical version of Ruby.

"Hawkner!" squeaked the apparition. She was summarily shoved through the door by a GQ model dressed in impeccably tailored shades of charcoal and lavender.

"Don't pause to narrate," he said as he slammed and locked the French doors. "Everybody down. She's right behind us."

Thomas watched the others dive under the table. After a moment, he shrugged and followed them. "Just out of curiosity, why are we terrified of Hawkner?"

Four people eyed him with varying degrees of disbelief.

"You're not from around here if you have to ask that," Felix said.

"I've lived here for almost a month." Thomas shrugged and banged his shoulder into the underside of the table. "Maybe she's avoiding me."

"Where?" Ruby inquired with more than casual interest.

"Down the street, in Random House."

"One of Gerry's friends. Supposed to be keeping an eye on Teddy?" Cerridwen asked.

"Yes."

"Well, there you go." The only other male under the table felt the mystery had been solved.

Thomas was still unenlightened.

"Teddy answered the door naked," Pearl explained. "Hawkner hasn't been back since."

Thomas tried very hard not to picture his eighty year old landlord in the nude. He was thankfully interrupted by Ruby.

"This is my sister Pearl, and Felix. Don't pay any attention to them. Neither of them is nearly as interesting as I am. The Hawkner is the over-achieving vice president of the Hysterical Society," explained Ruby, who had had the foresight to bring her cake with her. She went from one subject to the other and back again without pause. "She wants Cerridwen's house."

"And she thinks you're just going to give it to her?" Thomas hoped they weren't down here for long. He was not built to fit under tables.

"She doesn't want my house, really. She wants to run tours through it," Cerridwen said. "The rich history of Green Man Court, the characters that inhabited it, tourist attraction, yada, yada. Oh and something about money, blah blah."

"But why your house?"

"My grandmother passed away last year. The Hysterical—er, Historical Society had cherished hopes. Completely unfounded ones, as far as I can tell. But apparently it was a shock when it was all left to some upstart granddaughter lock, stock, and barrel."

"But, again, why your house?"

"A sort of living museum. But without the pesky people living in it," Felix answered. "Cerridwen's house has the most star power. Scandalous marriage between wealthy industrialist and exotic opera star resulting in an achingly expensive confection of a house. It was the top story in 1899, you know."

"Well, she can't have it," Cerridwen cut in. "It's in trust. I can't even sell, let alone hand it over to that avaricious society. Which I wouldn't anyways."

"Ideally she would rip mine right off its foundations. 1910 Italianate is so gauche. Of course, the story loses a little something when you learn that their torrid romance ended in a long, happy marriage and two beautiful children," Felix continued.

"Says you!" shot back the presumed Pearl. "It's a beautiful, romantic story."

"No drama in it," he countered with a shrug.

"Drama is Felix's middle name, you know," Ruby advised Thomas. "He writes historical fiction. His latest is something about a nymphomaniac Empress Theodosia and the Byzantine soldier that dared to meet her needs. It makes excellent bath time reading. And it's making him pots of money." She offered her sister a bite of cake with her fork. "What are you working on now, dear?" she asked Felix.

"A boy sets out from ancient Rome for Britain with a dream and a brick. A boy called Hadrian," replied Felix as he snagged a finger full of whipped cream from Ruby's plate.

"Did Hadrian ever go to Britain?" Thomas asked.

"No idea." Felix answered honestly. "It's historical fiction. Facts just get in the way of my brilliant re-imagining."

"That means that he makes shit up," Pearl threw in.

"Don't we all?" Cerridwen asked.

"But I make it up out of whole cloth. Like an honest person," Pearl shot back.

"Someone should explain to the latest acquisition to our group—you," Felix cut in. "You see, we all talk to our imaginary friends for a living."

Thomas turned to Cerridwen. "Imaginary friends?"

She smiled back at him. "Welcome to our Sunday afternoon writers' group. We're all mad here."

He studied her face, trying to figure out if she was serious. Also, it was a really nice face.

There was the sound of the front door creaking open. Everyone under the table froze, Ruby with her fork in her mouth, Felix with another finger full of cream halfway to his lips.

They waited breathlessly as footsteps approached. Sensible but stylish ballet flats and dark trousers appeared in their limited view of the doorway.

"Oh, it's only Jane," Cerridwen said with obvious relief.

Jane came into the kitchen, bent over and peered under the table. She studied them for a moment, with large, expressive eyes in an otherwise neutral expression. The music in Thomas head switched abruptly to the Harlem Nocturne. Jane was kind of hot if you liked older women who could kick your ass. Without a word she went to the fridge and retrieved a bottle of iced tea and then left. They could hear her pass through the foyer and up the grand staircase.

"And Jane is?" Thomas asked.

"My house mate. Homicide detective, night shift. More cake?'

* * * *

Thomas was thoughtful as he unlocked the door to Random House. For once the drumbeat was not in his head. He followed the sound into the front parlor. The once formal space was packed cheek by jowl with instruments including, directly in front of the fireplace, an eight piece drum kit.

Fred stopped pounding the drums when he saw Thomas. "How goes it?"

"I just met the girl I'm going to marry."

"Soundtrack?"

"Foreigner's greatest hits."

"Sweet."

Chapter 3

Cerridwen was furious. What a waste of a Tuesday night. Who planned a fundraiser for a Tuesday anyways? And to think that she had squandered her grandmother's red Schiaparelli evening dress on that atrocity called a party. She had never been so bored in her life. And, to add insult to injury Mrs. Gray, recently widowed light of Victorian society and current president of the dreaded Historical Society, had taken the opportunity go on and on about tracking down some table or other she wanted for a furniture exhibit.

"I could just as easily stayed home, stuck splinters under my fingernails, and had just as much fun," she informed the doorknob as she wrestled with the tarnished antique lock. It probably needed to be oiled again. Someday she would have it replaced, and damn the Historical Society, coveting people's furniture and having stupid rules about what she could and could not do to her house. And you could be damn sure when Mrs. Gray found that table, the "loan" she talked about would somehow become a gift. Cerridwen pitied anyone dumb enough to loan the Society anything.

She finally forced the door open. Her cell phone chose that moment to ring and Cerridwen swore in English, Welsh, and French as her beaded evening bag and keys hit the floor and skidded across the marble. The weight of the two and a half inch long brass key carried her keyring all the way under the table before it skidded to a stop.

"What, Gerry?" she snapped at the caller.

Her sometime cousin was unfazed. "Hey," Gerry said in a placid voice. "What ya doing?"

"Celebrating the death of a wretched party by flinging my possessions across my foyer." She found the light switch and scanned the floor as the chandelier flickered to life twenty feet above. She thought she had left it on, but the switch was in the off position. She made a note to check the connections. Would a tripped breaker have moved the switch? "What are you doing?"

"We're at the Gargoyle drinking Freddy's employee discount. Want to come help? I'm bored, Thomas is in a funk, and Fred's working."

The heavy scent of the heirloom carnations seemed stronger then this morning, when she had put them on the console table. "Why is Thomas in a funk? And who is Freddy?"

"Freddy is roommate slash Teddy minder number two. We're going to start a band. Well, Thomas and I are, and Fred is humoring us. And as for the other thing, my guess is because the president of the PTA wants to screw Thomas and you don't."

"Why does Thomas think I don't want to screw him?" Cerridwen hunted under the table for the key ring. From the sound of it, Gerry was fighting someone for possession of his phone.

"So you *do* want to screw Thomas?"

"I didn't say that. Ow." Her head hit the table edge.

"So you *don't* want to screw Thomas?"

"I'm not saying that either." She retrieved her keyring to a chorus of thumps and muffled voices.

"Ouch! Ouch! OK, whatever. Let go, Dude!" Gerry had won the fight for his phone. "So do you want to come eat nasty cheese fries or what?"

"I would love to. Let me change my clothes, find my keys, and figure out why my Chinese vase is in pieces on the floor, and—"

She felt rather than heard the dull thwack as something hit the back of her head. The inlaid marble floor rose alarmingly. She had just enough time to realize she was falling before everything went black.

* * * *

Something was beeping insistently. It was the kind of noise that would drive a woman to murder, and she should know.

And now someone was talking in the patient tone people used when they thought the person they were talking to was stupid. Cerridwen came to the conclusion that if she wanted the noise to stop, she would have to do something about it herself.

But, oh, her head hurt. With great effort, she pried one eye open. The first thing she saw was Jay Silverheels sprawled in a cramped plastic chair, staring at the florescent lights above him. Why the actor that played Tonto in the original *Lone Ranger* TV series was here, she couldn't fathom, but when she was more awake, she was going to ask him where he got the tattoo that covered most of his lower right arm.

Beside him, Gerry laid across a spinning stool, shifting his feet as he turned in a lazy, recumbent circle. Turning her head, she came face to face with Thomas, who had somehow wedged his bulk into the chair beside her.

"Apparently I am in a hospital," she told him. She was quite proud that she had worked this out for herself.

She located the source of the patient voice. A man in blue scrubs stood near the door. "I don't like him," she announced to the room and then let her eyes drift closed. "And the beeping needs to stop."

"The beeping is your heart monitor. And I was explaining to these gentlemen that visiting is supposed to be family only at this point."

"Brother," Tonto said to the ceiling.

"Cousin." Gerry made another slow circle.

"Fiancé." Thomas was matter of fact. In the context of Thomas and Gerry, she assumed Tonto must be Fred. Cerridwen wondered how she had missed getting engaged. She thought that was the kind of thing she would have remembered. Maybe if she was patient someone would explain it to her, but Blue Scrubs needed to go away. She was relieved in a detached sort of way when Jane breezed in with her professional face on.

"Everybody out," Jane said. Blue Scrubs displayed a smug smile until Jane gestured to the door. "You too." Shutting the door firmly on his protests, she turned to Cerridwen. "You want to tell me what happened?"

"You want to tell me? The last thing I remember, I was on the phone with Gerry. The vase was broken on the floor, and something hit me. And then I was here with a brand new family."

"I came home and found you on the floor. We don't know yet what you were hit with. It knocked you unconscious. You have a bit of a concussion." Jane looked toward the door where faint sounds of discord could be heard. "Those boys must have peeled out for the house before you hit the ground. They got there seconds after me. Beat the emergency vehicles by a full minute. And the ambulance only had to come from King Street."

"Gerry must have been driving."

"I know. And I have to say, I have my doubts about just how street legal that GTO is. Right now we're trying to figure out who hit you. My guess is they didn't think either of us would be home and the attack was spur of the moment. It doesn't get us very far, but it's a place to start."

Thoughts started to form behind the wall of fuzz and dizziness in Cerridwen's mind. "The dress I was wearing?" The clinging red satin had been replaced with a sickly green hospital gown.

"In the cabinet over there. I knew better than to let them cut you out of a vintage Schiaparelli evening dress."

With that worry out of the way, Cerridwen moved on to less important things. "My house?"

"The house is fine. Whoever it was only got as far as the library. No real damage, only minor casualties—the broken vase, a missing candlestick, and a little lacquered table. If it had drawers, I would have said they tried to open it. It should be fairly easy to put it back together.

The library seems to be the only room they entered. Any idea what they have been looking for?"

Cerridwen thought hard for a moment. The attempt underlined the throbbing pain in her head. That and a touch of dizziness were all she had to show for the effort. "Maybe they wanted to borrow a book? How did they get in?"

Jane eyed her worriedly. "We're not sure yet. No broken windows or jimmied doors. It would suggest either a picked lock or a key."

"You can't tell which?"

"No, contrary to popular belief. The only real way to tell is if they've scratched up the lock plate or left the tumblers out of place. If they're good, they don't do either. I think you need…"

The door burst open. The four men tumbled into the room, still arguing over the relative merits of imaginary family.

"I said," Jane continued in a louder voice. "You need to rest."

"That is just what I was saying." Blue Scrubs stuck in his oar.

"I can rest at home," she snapped. As soon as she got back to her computer she was writing him into a story and then murdering him with the most brutal method she could devise.

"You can't go home yet," Mr. Smug Scrubs retorted. "You have a concussion and you have to be monitored until we're sure you're out of danger."

Boiling oil. Defiantly boiling oil. A whole bubbling vat of it. Did health inspectors wear scrubs?

"You told me it was a 'mild' concussion." Jane had her interrogation face on now.

"In as much as something like this can be called mild."

"So she can go home if someone stays with her?" Jane plucked the chart out of his hand and flipped through it.

"Well, yes. But—"

"I assume you can provide discharge instructions that, if followed, would lessen any danger to the patient?"

"Of course we could, but…"

"So it would be perfectly reasonable to send her home in the care of her cousin?" She looked questioningly at the three young men.

"Second cousins once divorced," offered Gerry.

"Her brother?"

"Twin, actually." Cerridwen presumed this was Fred. "By different parents."

"And her fiancé?" Jane raised her eyebrows at Thomas.

"Planning ahead. Or wishful thinking, take your pick."

Jane gave Thomas a hard stare and then continued. "Take Cerridwen home. Stay the night. The three of you take it in shifts if you have to. I'll be home between six and seven a.m. Call my cell if you need me. You get her stuff." She pointed at Scrub Boy. "Everybody out while she gets dressed."

"You're sending her home with her imaginary boyfriend?" Gerry asked.

"You think I didn't run a background check as soon as I found him under the kitchen table?"

"Well, now you're just making him sound like a stalker," Fred interjected.

"You checked me out?" Thomas was torn between irritated and flattered.

"Relax, sugar. I just looked for criminal history, or lack thereof, as it turned out. I didn't do anything that school you work for hadn't already done. By the time Ruby was done, she knew what size underwear you wear. Now let's go, boys. Out."

Thomas, Fred, and Gerry responded in unison with a resounding "Yes, ma'am." They ushered the dissenter out of the room by the simple means of walking towards him till he had to move or be stepped on.

Jane followed them. "And I want to talk to you, Gerry, about that car."

Chapter 4

The intricate plaster ceiling informed Cerridwen that she had fallen asleep in the grand salon. Thomas was asleep next to her, taking up three quarters of the settee and causing a crater in the process. Sometime in the night he had thrown an arm across her.

She struggled out from under it. The man had arms like a damn oak tree! And apparently a tattoo—interesting. She took a moment to study the tiny two inch ravens, five of them scattered from collar bone to shoulder.

The clock said it was a quarter to noon, but it felt like the morning after the apocalypse. Cerridwen's head still throbbed. Her memory of last night was a fog of dizziness and nausea broken by the sound of well-meaning voices and B movies. They woke her up every hour or so to ask her name, the date, the president, etc. following that damn ER doctor's orders.

Boiling oil was too good for that damned doctor. What about those machines they used to dehydrate beef jerky? Would those scrubs shrivel with him? You really had to get the details right on something like that.

Dimly she noticed that it was raining again, and she needed to check if the century old window frames were leaking. The TV blasted mid-afternoon reruns at the now silent room. Long and lanky Gerry was asleep on the floor. The compact Fred oozed off the chaise lounge at an alarming angle, showing slightly more animation in this state than he had awake. She had a full house. She wondered if any of them had remembered to call into work.

Cerridwen padded out to the hall. She turned on the computer to see what the internet had to say about jerky making. She had a murder to plan.

* * * *

Thomas wasn't sure what woke him up. He thought it might have been the lack of Cerridwen's steady breathing that dragged him to the surface. Or it could have been the lack of 80s power ballads that played in his head whenever she was near. He stretched and rolled over. Well, he tried to roll over, but what he really did was fall off the couch and clip his shoulder on the coffee table.

Fred groaned. Gerry pulled a throw pillow over his head. Thomas picked himself up and made a colorful suggestion regarding the ancestry of the furniture in question. It was just not made for someone his size, but few things were. He spent a few moments looking for his shirt before he remembered Cerridwen had been sick on it sometime last night.

Rubbing his shoulder, he padded barefoot and shirtless out to the hall. He was hoping she hadn't gotten far. Cerridwen had spent her wakeful periods puking and inserting obscenities into the prosaic answers to date of birth and what year was it. She had an impressive vocabulary.

The faint sound of music guided him down the hall toward the back of the house. The marble was cool against his feet as he followed the sound of the Sherilles through the kitchen into Cerridwen's tidy little office. She didn't notice him at first. He took a moment to have a staring contest with her iPod as "Will You Still Love Me Tomorrow" blared into the little room. He snatched it off the desk top and scrolled through it till he found what he wanted. The music suddenly changed to When In Rome's "The Promise."

The change in music was the first sign that he was in the room. He could be shockingly silent when he wanted to be.

Cerridwen looked at the iPod in his hand and then at him. "What's that supposed to mean?"

"What do you think it means?" He cocked an eyebrow.

"You know, there are women the world over that would kill for those eyebrows."

Both brows shot up.

"And those eyelashes. Women pay good money for fake ones half as long."

"Off topic," he pointed out.

"It's where I live most of the time."

"I know. I think it's part of your appeal."

"Speaking of my appeal—fiancé?" she asked.

"They wouldn't let me in to see you unless I was family." He shrugged.

"Fiancé?" She questioned again.

"I panicked." He sighed. "We're friends, right? So we can be honest with each other."

"It's hard to say no after I tossed my cookies down your shirt."

"Well, it was part panic, part wishful thinking. I will back off if you don't feel the same way. But there is a line between friends and more than friends. And we are headed straight for it. I just want it clear that if we cross that line you are stuck with me. For good, possibly for life."

"I think I'm OK with that," she said after a moment of thought. He was going to say something more, but the doorbell rang like a shrill scream. He sighed again and set the iPod on the desk.

He made the long trek to the front door and opened it mid-shriek. "And now I'm deaf," he told the woman on the other side. Well-preserved was the phrase that sprang to his mind. The premature gray hair and black turtle neck were an interesting combination against the full flowered skirt and the deceptively simple strains of Pachelbel's

"Canon in D" he heard in his mind as he looked at her. He was amused to note the assessing look she gave him. But he was more interested in the basket on one of her arms that smelled like warm bread.

"Joan Witt." She thrust a slim callused hand at him. "And you are?"

"Thomas Rakmelevich." He shook her hand. It was surprisingly strong for a woman her size.

"Do you know you don't have a shirt on?"

"I am aware, yes."

"Nice tattoo." She breezed past him into the house.

"Come on in," he said to the empty air. "Bad time? Nope. Not at all. Not like my love life is important or anything. Hell, it's practically nonexistent at this point." He shut the door and followed Joan.

She knew her way to the kitchen without any help—sailed in as if she owned the place. He might have been upset by this if she hadn't chosen that moment to reveal that the basket was full of croissants.

Briefly he considered throwing her out and keeping the croissants. Instead, he inched around her into Cerridwen's office, sliding the pocket door closed behind him.

"Joan Witt is in your kitchen. She brought food."

Cerridwen jerked upright, scattering sticky notes. "Joan is here? Don't let her in here! She *cleans.*" The last word was uttered in a tone reserved for only the most heinous of crimes. She grabbed her notebook and ran for the other door. "Tell her I'm in the dining room. And lock the door on your way out."

Thomas turned, nearly colliding with Joan. He reached back to make sure the lock had clicked. "Cerridwen is in the dining room," he said.

"But I thought—"

"Dining room."

"Oh, well. If you say so."

He followed her for a simple reason: she had taken the croissants with her.

The dining room was an Art Nouveau wonderland that seemed to be carved from a single piece of honey-toned maple. He forgot about breakfast for a moment as he stared at the portrait dominating the wall above the fireplace. Yards and yards of blue silk surrounded the subject while doing nothing to conceal her spectacular figure. A headdress of jeweled peacock feathers drew attention to her face. At first, he thought it was Cerridwen, but then he noticed the eyes were darker, the skin paler. The nose was a little sharper and the expression was a tad more knowing. He was going to ask Cerridwen if this was the famous, opera-singing great-grandmother, but Joan was already filling the room with words.

"Cerridwen, I came as soon as I heard. You'd think I would have heard all the commotion last night, but it's like living in a monastery back there behind Great Grand Daddy's wall. Silent as the grave, I tell you. I had no idea what had happened until I met Mr. Deets at the bakery this morning. The horrid little man has a police scanner apparently." Sitting at the table and buttering croissants, she never seemed to pause for breath.

"Such a thing to happen. I just can't imagine. What could they have been after? Do you have any idea? And to attack you like that." It wasn't a rapid spat of words. The tempo was fairly mellow; there were just no breaks in the flow. It reminded Thomas strongly of beat poetry.

The doorbell made its unholy presence known once more. Thomas went to answer it, Joan's voice following him through the house. The horrifically historical sound rang out twice more before he yanked open the door.

The woman on the other side was a study in contrasts. She desperately wanted to be Jackie O but had landed, badly, somewhere near a poor man's Nancy Reagan. The assessing look she gave him was cold, hard, and calculating. It lacked the warmth of Joan's earlier gesture. Thomas found it oddly irritating.

"Young man, you are not wearing a shirt," she snapped.

"It has been mentioned."

"That is an entirely inappropriate way to answer the door. Particularly a door that is not your own." She looked down her nose at him. No easy feat considering he was nearly two feet taller than her.

"Well, that's a chance you take with doors. You never know when there will be a half-naked man on the other side."

"I don't know what you are implying, but I don't care for it, I can tell you that much."

"Really?" Thomas feigned surprise. "'Cause Ruby would have grabbed on that chance with both hands. Hell, Ruby would have grabbed me with both hands."

His new acquaintance stuck her nose even higher in the air, if that was possible. Her nostrils pinched as if she smelled something foul, and she stomped past him. She eyed the cavernous entry with more affection than she probably ever showed a living person. He would have called it avarice if it wasn't for the strangely erotic way she stroked the banister as she passed it.

"Ann Hawkner, I presume."

"Young man, I don't know who you are or why you are wandering around this house half dressed. But I tell you I mean to find out!" She paused long enough to squawk indignantly at Fred and Gerry still sleeping in the grand salon. She rushed into the dining room. Thomas shrugged and went after her.

"Miss Evan Jones, I wish to speak to you!" Did the woman speak in nothing but indignation and exclamation points? It was having a bad effect on his internal soundtrack. It was all "Ride of The Valkyries" since she walked in the door. "How was this break-in allowed to occur? Why was the house not better safe guarded?"

Cerridwen didn't even look up from her notes. She had spread a notebook and a sheaf of papers on the table, an illustration of the saying on her tank top: "I'm plotting against you in my novel." It contrasted oddly with the black silk jammie pants and the vintage kimono.

"Hello, Ms. Hawkner. I'm fine, by the way. Thanks for asking."

"But the house! How did he get in the house? How could this have happened? Perhaps I should take this up with the trustees!"

"You do that. And while you're there, be sure to mention that the locks are more than a hundred years old and there is no security system because you and the rest of the Historical Society felt it would damage the integrity of the house." She glanced at her empty teacup as if she wasn't sure where it came from, or why it was empty.

Joan stuck a croissant in her hand and took the teacup. "These things happen, Ann. It's not something that Cerridwen, or even your Historical Society, has any control over. All we can do is chalk it up to experience and fix what damage we can." She fussed with the tea things.

"Damage? There was damage to the house?" It looked as if Ms. Hawkner was about to have a stroke.

"No, there was no damage to *my* house," Cerridwen said "Just my head and one of the Chinese vases. Thank you so much for your concern." Her voice was just a little tart.

"Something similar happened at Whitmore, Cerridwen, just before your grandmother passed away. Oh, more than a year ago now. Didn't take anything—just shuffled, around opening drawers and such. Almost as if they were sightseeing. Of course, if we'd been home at the time, who knows what would have happened." Joan arranged cups and plates as she talked.

"It's a scandal," Ms. Hawkner whispered as if Joan hadn't spoken. "People charging in and out and breaking things at will. Men running the halls half naked. The whole tone of the neighborhood is running downhill rapidly. Who are these men I find all over the house, if I might ask?" It didn't sound at all like a question.

"Isn't it obvious, Ann? I'm having an orgy."

Miss Hawkner gasped and dropped into a chair. Thomas couldn't decide if she was horrified by the word orgy, or the use of her first name. He leaned toward the latter. Ann Hawkner had probably had a wild youth. Cerridwen went back to ignoring her.

"Oh, it's not as bad as all that. She just let a few friends stay the night." Joan laughed.

"And how is this going to affect the tours?" Ms. Hawkner fiddled with her pearls.

"It won't affect them at all. Because I still haven't agreed to them." Cerridwen didn't even look up this time.

"A little scandal never hurt anyone," Joan said.

"Well, of course you would think that, wouldn't you? But with your history, I suppose you would have to." Miss Hawkner waved a hand dismissively.

"And what is that supposed to mean?" Joan's eyes narrowed.

"Just that scandal is bread and butter to some people. Especially when you turn that scandal into a book deal," Hawkner snapped.

"Oh, for God's sake, what are you rambling about now?" Cerridwen was losing patience with all the distractions.

"Haven't you heard? The famed Michael Stone is writing a biography of Thaddeus Witt. Joan is letting him spread all the Witt's dirty laundry out on the lawn for fun and profit."

"That is an oversimplification at best. And at worst it's just plain mean, Ann." Joan's voice was calm.

"Are we to assume that there isn't some kind of compensation involved?" Hawkner's replied snidely.

"There is some money involved, of course. Mr. Stone has agreed to donating part of the proceeds from the book sales to Whitmore House's restoration. But it's really more about the history of the place and the lives that were touched by Whitmore. And by Daddy, of course. And is publicity such a bad thing? It might even give your little society a bit of a boost." It was a subtle dig, but it was still enough to make Hawkner bristle.

"Not all publicity is good publicity. We can't all ride out the tide of public opinion on the wake of our family's former glory. This is not 1965. And we are not dealing with a disappearing dance hall girl!" Ms. Hawkner snapped. Joan jerked back like she'd been slapped.

Cerridwen surfaced from her muttering and note taking to stare at Hawkner. Her silvery gray eyes were hard and cold as she pointed her pen at the offender. "Why are you here, Ms. Hawkner? It's certainly not out of concern for my safety. And as the house is still standing, there really doesn't seem to be anything here for you to do."

"I was speaking to Mrs. Gray yesterday." Hawkner drew herself up to her full height. Her hand went to her pearls again. She pulled at them and then patted them back into place, running her fingers down the strand. "She is very excited about the idea of tours here at Witt's

End. She and I would like to make them part of Victoria's upcoming Founder's Day celebration."

"How very sad it must be for both of you, knowing that is not going to happen." Cerridwen turned back to her notes.

"A landmark like this really should have been put into the hands of the Historical Society, or at the very least the city." Ms. Hawkner addressed the portrait of Cerridwen's great-grandmother. "But blood will out. I don't suppose you can expect the descendants of an opera singer to have a sense of history any more than you can expect a cabbage to turn into a rose."

"That was uncalled for. And your metaphors are laborious and clunky." It was unclear which Cerridwen thought was the greater crime. "I think you should leave now."

The Nancy Reagan clone twitched, lifting her hand. *My God,* Thomas thought, *she's clutching her pearls. I didn't know people really did that.* She opened her mouth, thought better of it, and turned sharply, leaving the room, her kitten heels clicking against the stone floors she so admired.

The unflappable Joan slumped in her chair and the color drained from her face. "Why on earth would she bring up Mary Paul?"

"The 60s are on her mind lately. Ever since she found out that my great-grandmother and grandmother kept diaries, she's been after me to donate them to the museum. Their historical value must be greater than their scandalous content, unless she means to edit them. That and Stone writing your father's bio and the stupid graffiti. And the scandal isn't quite old enough to gain any polish in her eyes. Thank God no one told her it was the library that was ransacked. Her head would have popped."

"Are you sure it wasn't her?" Thomas asked. "I could see her putting on a ninja mask and 'liberating' some of the more historical of your possessions in a daring rescue mission."

Cerridwen laughed. "She probably would if she thought of it. For their own good, of course."

"For the good of history," he corrected her.

"What is this about graffiti?" Joan sat up and fiddled with the tea things. She lined up the spoons and then stacked them.

"Someone has been spray painting 'Where Did Mary Go?' around town. Teddy said that appeared after Mary Paul's disappearance, also. I wouldn't think it has any connection, though. It has been a long time." Cerridwen shrugged, dismissing it and anything else that didn't have to do with her plot.

"She mentioned the diary the other day," Joan said. "That must be why the rant about the morals of 'artistic types' was long in coming this morning. It was uncharacteristically brief."

"Good thing she didn't know I was wearing red last night," Cerridwen said. "She wouldn't have been able to resist the scarlet woman analogy."

Joan froze for a moment, her eyes widened. Then she threw her head back and laughed. It was a full, ringing sound. But it struck Thomas's musical ear that the laugh was edging dangerously close to cracking.

She gathered her basket and her boho bag, her hand trembling slightly. "I'm sorry, but I think I need to go. I need to clear my head after...I just can't imagine why she would bring up Mary after all these years." Joan sighed. "I'm sorry, it's just very upsetting."

Joan turned towards the front of the house to leave. Thomas followed her. There were far too many people wandering in and out of this place for his peace of mind.

Chapter 5

Cerridwen took a deep breath. Now, just maybe, she could get five minutes of work done.

Ruby catapulted into the room with Pearl close behind. No, she wouldn't be getting any work done in the near future. Virginia Woolf had been right. She needed a room of her own. Maybe a padded cell. With a lock on the inside.

"What on Earth went on here last night?" Ruby came from the back of the house, having presumably waltzed in through the kitchen. Pearl bobbed along behind like a balloon on a string. "Police, ambulance, Jane three feet off the ground. And poor Thomas, white as a sheet. Hello, Thomas. You're not wearing a shirt."

Thomas stared down at himself. "Oh my God. How did that happen? Where did it go? How could I have not noticed?" He tossed it off in a conversational tone as he reached for the tea pot.

Pearl continued to stare at him. "Nice tattoo," she offered in way of greeting.

"Thank you. A couple of people have mentioned that this morning." There was a rattle of china and the clink of metal. Cerridwen looked up as Thomas set down her now filled teacup at her elbow. She sniffed the Lipton black pearl that she drank when she had no one else to please. “Oh, you’re good,” she told him.

He smiled faintly but didn’t look at her as he handed her the sugar bowl. “Why does the name Mary Paul send everyone around here into fits?” he asked as he lowered himself carefully into the dining chair as if afraid it wouldn’t take his weight. It creaked in protest beneath him.

Pearl and Ruby froze in mid croissant raid to stare at him, wide eyed.

“Yeah.” He pointed. “Just like that.”

“We’re just surprised that you don’t know.” Ruby slathered butter on her croissant. “It’s one of Victoria’s few claims to fame. Some people called the crime of the century. Which I think is odd since it was never proven there was a crime.”

“All atmosphere, no plot,” Pearl interrupted. “Have you heard of the Prophet Witt?”

“I’m not particularly interested in religion,” Thomas answered.

Pearl made a face at him. The butter smeared across her top lip somewhat lessened the effect. “The psychic, Joan’s father. They called him the Prophet Witt. Silly name. He went into some sort of trance or something. Kind of like that Edgar Cayce. Cayce was quite the rage in his time.”

“I never understood his appeal,” Ruby interrupted again. “All that fuss over a man who just talked in his sleep.”

Thomas fixed them both with a hard stare. Cerridwen suddenly understood how he was able to control a room full of kindergartners. Ruby subsided with a bit of a sulk.

“When he met Mary Paul it was—well, I’m not sure what it was. I would have called it lust at first sight. But it wasn’t really. It was too cerebral. I’m not sure what it was. He called her his muse. And she moved into the house. It was a bit of scandal. God knows why, with the house practically a commune as it was. Something like thirty people already clinging to his coattails.”

"Pearl. You know why it was a scandal. Mary was an actress." Ruby stressed the last word heavily.

"What has that to do with anything?" her sister snapped.

"It was the 60s. Actress still equaled prostitute in some people's minds—especially in small towns like Victoria. Movies as art was still a new concept." Ruby's strained but patient tone made Cerridwen wonder if Ruby had experienced this prejudice first hand.

"That is ridiculous. The movies were mainstream by that point," Thomas interjected.

"And it made a difference to the stars on the top tier. But those of us still in the trenches were not painted with the same glamorous brush, I assure you." Ruby shrugged.

"Well, it was little more than a nine days' wonder until she disappeared. Off the face of the earth." Pearl made a sweeping gesture with one hand. "And that in itself might not have made such a noise. But Witt claimed that she had ascended to heaven. He said he had seen it. Gave quite the description. The general assumption was that he had killed her and was trying to cover it up. I think that if he had he would have come up with a better story."

"But why tell the story in the first place?" Cerridwen asked. "Or why tell any story? Why not just pass it off?"

"But he didn't make it up," Pearl corrected her. "At least not consciously."

"I don't understand," Thomas said.

"Drugs, dear. Open secret at the time. That's how he had his visions. It was something about the tea he was always pushing. He called it herbal. And it may have been, for all I know. But there was something in there that carried quite a wallop was the rumor."

"I always assumed it was one of his hangers-on that helped Mary disappear," Ruby offered.

"Competition?" asked Thomas.

"I couldn't say for sure. It was a very strange time over at Witt's house. All those weird people, and that's coming from me! And all the while the house crumbling around them and the gardens going to pot.

Of course, it takes a fair bit to feed that many people and not a job between them. But Witt talked Mary into moving in and it wasn't a month later somebody did for her."

"We don't know that they killed her. She just disappeared. And no one agrees on how or even when," Pearl said. "There are about a dozen conflicting stories, everything from she just left, to her body being hidden somewhere in Whitmore."

"The authorities didn't seem to care. I always wondered why one of you didn't write about it," Ruby said.

"No romance," Pearl answered.

"No body," Cerridwen chimed in.

"And Felix?" Thomas asked.

"Too new," Pearl offered.

"Really? I would have said the story didn't have enough sex in it," Cerridwen commented.

Thomas stared at her. "I would have thought a story like that had plenty of sex in it."

"Have you read his books? Historic sex with some plot thrown in for flavor."

Any further conversation on Felix's narrative style or Mary Paul's disappearance was forestalled by the thud of feet. Gerry stumbled in blurry-eyed, Fred close behind.

"Caffeine," Fred pronounced. So far, he was a man of few and infrequent words.

"They don't have coffee. You'll have to make do with black tea," Thomas told him. This was answered by incredulous mumbling and a sound that may have been soft weeping.

A fully dressed and wide awake Jane breezed into the room with her usual air of easy competence. "Good Morning. Cerridwen. You can get in the library today, if you want to tidy up. Thomas, you're not wearing a shirt."

Thomas looked down at himself. "Oh my God! Where is my shirt? How did this happen?" he exclaimed in mock horror.

Jane waited, expressionless.

Thomas shrugged. "It's in the wash. Cerridwen puked on it last night. And you are the fourth person to mention it."

"Jane, dear, where are you going?" Pearl asked.

"Work."

"You just got off work." Cerridwen pointed out.

"Split shift. Be good, children. Try not to bring the neighborhood to its knees until I get back from work."

"Is she talking to us?" Gerry asked Fred.

Pearl thought on this for a moment. "I rather thought she was talking to us girls."

"Why do you have a portrait of yourself in your dining room?" Fred asked Cerridwen, pointing at the painting on the far wall.

"It's not me, it's my great grandmother," she answered.

"The one he built the house for?" Thomas asked.

"Yes." She didn't look up, flipping through the papers on the table in pursuit of a particular sticky note.

Fred eyed the painting consideringly. "I'd would've built her a house, too."

Chapter 6

It was well into the afternoon before the cleanup effort in the library began in earnest. Ruby and Pearl had taken themselves off in a cloud of chiffon shortly after Jane's departure. Fred and Gerry were willing enough, but not sure exactly how to go about cleaning up a two-story library. Thankfully the damage was superficial. All of the drawers and cabinets had been searched and then closed again. The books pulled off the shelves were neatly stacked on the floor in front of the built-in bookcases. Apparently Cerridwen's vandal had OCD.

In the light of day it looked as if someone had attempted to read every book in the room. No, realized Cerridwen, not every book. She sat down on the Aubusson carpet and chased the thought that slipped just out of reach.

Thomas, wearing a newly laundered tee shirt, found her sprawled in a beam of afternoon sunshine, tracing the intricate pattern of birds and flowers with her finger. She had on what he had come to think off as her plotting face, with her eyes narrowed as she chewed her lip.

"Aren't you supposed to be 'tidying?'" he asked her.

She stretched out on her back and gazed up at him from the floor. The gold on black kimono spread out around her, clashing with the equally exotic carpet. "Aren't you supposed to be teaching music appreciation to sixth graders? It's Wednesday."

"I called in this morning. They got a sub. Or sent them to study hall. Or let them loose to fling poo at the local populace." He dropped down on the carpet beside her. "Wow. That's a hell of a ceiling. Is that real gold?"

"Gold leaf. It's a bitch to clean."

"It looks it."

"You should see the music room sometime...and I am thinking," Cerridwen said.

"I can tell."

She poked him in the side. "Don't interrupt. I am thinking, what do all those books have in common?"

"Well," Gerry said as he came to sprawl beside them. "They're your books."

"That can't be it," Fred said, joining them. He had the forethought to drop a throw pillow on the floor before he lay down. This excellent idea was foiled when Cerridwen yanked it out from under his head and tucked it under her own. "Ow. If it was just books that belonged to her, they would all be on the floor."

Gerry reached out and pulled one long kimono sleeve across his face like a silk mustache. "There are enough on floor as it is. Are they on the same subject?"

"Not so much," Fred told the gilt cherubs above them.

"Same publisher?" Thomas offered.

"That's it!" Cerridwen surged off the carpet, dislodging bodies as she went. Gerry rolled out of the way with practiced ease. Thomas gave an oof of surprise, and Fred took the opportunity to retrieve the throw pillow.

She ran to one of the piles of books left haphazardly on the floor. “Account book, Aunt Eva’s household hints, great grandfather’s travel log. They are all the same.”

“Aunt Eva’s household hints?” Fred inquired.

“Hey, don’t knock it. You never know when you’ll have to roast a flamingo.”

“How are they the same?” Thomas eyed the travel log with distrust.

“They’re all unpublished. Most of them have blank spines.” Cerridwen started to gather books on the table.

“Some of them have dates on the spine,” Gerry said.

“This one has initials.” Fred retrieved one from under the table. For the next hour they gathered books and stacked them on the table. Every one of the books that had been pulled from the shelves was unpublished, the majority of them handwritten, a very few with marked spines. At the end there were more than a hundred books piled on the table.

“So other than being unpublished and in my possession, what do these books have in common?” Cerridwen said.

“Do they share subject matter?” Fred asked.

“No, they’re all something different. They share weirdness, if that’s anything,” Thomas said.

“Well, if a rare weird book collector was going to plan a heist, this would be the place,” Gerry said.

“No, the place would be *your* house. Teddy has more weird stuff than I could ever hope to possess.”

“Yeah, but at Random House you run the risk of seeing Teddy naked. Here there’s just a cop and a crazy lady that murders her imaginary friends,” Fred pointed out.

“And the chance to see Cerridwen naked,” Gerry added.

“Dude, you are doing a very bad job of pretending to be her cousin,” Thomas said, glaring.

"I am actually her cousin. Teddy and her grandmother were married for six months in 1968. Which makes her my second cousin once divorced. Which is totally a thing."

Cerridwen ignored them entirely. "The books that have years on them." She thought for a moment. "What years are they?"

Fred shuffled books for a moment before answering. "They are all from the 1960s. Most from 1965."

"So what happened in the 1960s that someone thinks they will find in my library?" She was interrupted by a silvery chime.

Thomas looked up from a hardbound auction catalog of antique instruments he had found in the drifts of books on the floor. "That is not the doorbell." He spoke with the voice of experience.

"No, it's the clock," Cerridwen answered absently.

Fred craned around to look at the gilded clock face. "It's time for Ginger to drive me to work." He poked Gerry.

"And time for you to use your employ discount to buy me some cheese fries." Gerry searched for his keys.

"Cheaper than gas money," Fred answered as they left.

Cerridwen retrieved a piece of paper and a pen from the writing desk under the window. On one side she made a list of the books they had found on the floor. On the other she made a list of things that had happened in the 1960s. She started with Mary's disappearance, but only got as far as Constance Frey marries. Her grandmother had been ten years older than Teddy.

She turned to look at Thomas. The chair he sat in was too low for him to bend his knees comfortably, so his legs stretched across the carpet.

"Thomas, how old are you?"

"Twenty-six," he answered.

Cerridwen made a choking noise. He glanced up and then back down at the catalog.

"I am thirty," she told him.

"That's nice."

"In November I will turn thirty-one."

"That is generally the way birthdays work. Do you think that I can afford a seventeenth century pianoforte?"

"No. And that catalog is more than forty years old. The instruments in it are all in private collections by now. Did you know?"

He looked up. "That I can't afford an antique piano?"

"No!" she answered sharply.

"That you're older than me? No, but I don't see that it makes a difference. I still plan to marry you when I grow up."

For the first time in a long time Cerridwen was dumbfounded.

"Now that that's settled," he said, throwing the catalog on the table. "What do you say we have pizza for dinner?"

Chapter 7

Cerridwen had come to a horrible realization. She'd spent days writing and rewriting, but the plot still didn't work. The only way to solve her problem was with another dead body. Ann, Norland's sister would have to die. The only question was when and where.

No, that wasn't right. She knew when. It would have to be before Norland's arrest but, of course, after his wife's death. Maybe shortly after the funeral, she decided. Yes, Ann really needed to die. How to kill Ann was the question now.

She'd already used stabbing. It had a certain elegance. But Hal was trying to cover up his first crime. Hanging was difficult to fake. Strangling was too obvious. He would want something that looked like an accident. After all, he still thought he was going to get away with it.

Cerridwen was weighing poison against drowning when Thomas appeared in the doorway of her office. Filled the doorway was maybe a better description.

Over the past week she had become accustomed to Gerry and his friends wandering through her house in shifts. She suspected "keep an eye on Cerridwen" had been added to the 'to do' list somewhere between "make sure Teddy is wearing pants" and "shoot the Hawkner on sight." She might have noticed him sooner, but the flower arrangement taking up half her desk also blocked her view of the door.

He eyed the spindle legged chair on the other side of her desk. He thought better of it and dropped into the wing chair by the window. Perhaps she should invest in some bigger furniture.

"Where did that come from?" He gestured at the overflowing vase.

"It's from Felix. He's gone on book tour and didn't hear about the head wound until yesterday."

"It's a bit over the top." He waved his hand in front of him as if beating away carnivorous foliage.

"Felix is all about the over-the-top gesture. What day is it? I thought you were working."

"It's Sunday. I don't have classes on Sunday."

"I thought it was Friday. No, it was Friday. About two chapters ago."

"You mean you haven't slept at all?" He frowned. "You are supposed to be resting. You're still recovering from a concussion."

"I've slept some. Sleep is for people not staring a deadline in the face. And I've had a lot to think about." She didn't tell him he was one of the things she had been thinking about. No need to stroke his ego.

Maybe she could arrange for a car accident for Ann. Huh, she had given Norland's sister-in-law Hawkner's first name. She hadn't noticed that before. "And not much time to do it. How do you feel about asphyxiation?"

"Generally, I'm against it. But if it's anyone other than me, I'm all for it. If you're quite done killing imaginary people for the moment, how about lunch? Ruby says this week's meeting is a picnic under the Green Man. And I have been ordered to fetch you."

She turned from the computer and blinked at him. "It's October."

"It's warm today. And she wants to have 'one last fling,' she says."

Cerridwen laughed. "Ruby Sands will have a last fling right before her last breath. And between now and then she will have as many as she wants. It is the nature of the Sands' sisters." She saved, saved again just to be sure, and then closed the file she had been working on. She hit save obsessively. It was very nearly a nervous habit. She lived in dread of losing all her work. "But by all means, let's go have a picnic. Especially since I suspect that it is at least partially for my benefit."

Ruby never did anything by halves. She had gotten Fred and Gerry to carry tables out on to the green angle of land between the houses. Heavens knew where she had found the tables. The chairs were from Teddy's Hepplewhite dining set. *If the Hawkner sees that,* thought Cerridwen, *she will fling herself upon them shrieking "No, take me instead!"*

Teddy sat in one near the lilacs looking about him with a lively air that would easily have him passing for seventy instead of well into his 90s. Fred and Gerry were rearranging furniture as Ruby directed them with dramatic gestures of her cider glass from her seat under the oak. They were lucky she hadn't demanded they move the folly or the fountain. But then the day was young yet.

Thomas went to help and Cerridwen dropped into the chair beside Ruby.

"Is all this for me?" she asked.

"Well, not all of it, dear," Ruby said. "I will admit to an attempt to get you out of the house. But the strapping young men moving furniture is purely for aesthetic reasons. And I figured Thomas had more chance of getting you out of your lair. No, no, boys, other way round." Ruby waved her glass at them.

"I do have a deadline to meet," Cerridwen pointed out. Even she could hear the faint sulk in her voice.

"And you will work it out at the last second, just like Pearl. Probably with a brilliant twist ending that came to you in the shower. That's what Pearl usually does."

"Pearl writes romances," Cerridwen said. "Her brilliant twist ending is that they end up together in the end."

"Yes, but she always makes you think they won't."

"Where is Pearl?"

"Oh, she'll be along. She's having a lovers' spat. They have to have two more fights before the end of the book, and that means all kinds of makeup sex, you know."

Joan came through Whitmore's massive front gate carrying her ubiquitous basket of baked goods. She was arm and arm with a stranger as her son, Jason, trailed reluctantly behind them. The fair-haired stranger was wearing the pseudo-intellectual uniform of dark slacks and tweed coat. He eyed the group under the trees with the expectant air of someone looking to be entertained. Jason, in his jeans and sturdy work shirt, detached himself and his mother's basket to join the three younger men moving tables.

There was mutiny in the ranks as the four of them decided there would be no more shifting. They converged on the table and demanded food. Through it all, Jason studiously ignored his mother's guest. Joan, perversely, seemed all the more proud and possessive of her guest.

"Ruby, Cerridwen. You must meet Michael. Ruby Sands, Cerridwen Evan Jones, this is Michael Stone." Joan performed proper introductions.

"Evan-Jones." He ran it together, making it one word. "The daughter of Liam Jones and Claudia Evans, both exceptional acting talents."

Why did people always feel the need to tell her who her parents were? She assumed that it was to assure themselves they were social climbing in the right direction. They couldn't really think she didn't know who her parents were.

"Michael Stone, the biographer?" Ruby felt the sudden chill and jumped into the breach. "I've read your books. Some of them were even about people that I knew."

"Ruby Sands, the actress? I would love to hear the stories you have to tell. You've had such an interesting career."

"You flatter me, dear. As long as you just don't mention how long a career." Ruby laughed. "But what on Earth are you doing here?" She reached over and dragged a dining chair across the grass, its antique legs making grooves in the manicured sod. "Sit down and tell me all about it." Mr. Stone was no match for Ruby's practiced gushing.

"I'm researching a biography of Thaddeus Witt. Joan has been kind enough to let me stay at Whitmore. It will let me get a good feel for who Thaddeus was and give me a better picture of his day-to-day life. It's a pity that more of his followers aren't still around. Nothing beats a firsthand account." He settled into the chair next to Ruby, prepared to hold forth.

Joan sat on his other side. "Unfortunately, with Daddy gone, there was not a lot of reason for them to stay. They've all moved on with their lives. I know where some of them are, but not all. And, of course, some of them have passed on. His work interested people of all ages." Her eyes misted.

"The place must seem a bit empty these days," Ruby offered sympathy.

"Very empty." Joan wiped her eyes. "And falling down around my ears. It takes a bit of effort to maintain that Gothic pile. And Daddy's books don't sell as they used to."

"Perhaps I can help a bit with that. A well marketed biography might raise some interest. And the metaphysical is a big seller right now." Mr. Stone polished his glasses thoughtfully. "And then, of course, there is the mystery angle."

"Whatever do you mean by mystery?" Joan asked, distracted by the arrival of Pearl and a mound of whipped cream that might or might not have contained cake.

"Mary Paul's disappearance. By all accounts, it is still unsolved." He stood and took the plate from Pearl. He would have set it on the table, but was intercepted by Fred with a hungry look in his eye.

Pearl retrieved the treat and handed Fred, instead, a large, greasy grocery bag. "Fried chicken. You are expected to share," she called after him as he bore the bag off with howls of victory.

“It was, of course, quite upsetting for everyone at the time,” Joan brushed off the incident. “But it didn’t have any real impact on Daddy’s message, or his method.”

Cerridwen wondered how the disappearance of anyone could have no real impact. But the thought was put aside as chairs were rearranged one last time before everyone settled around Teddy’s oak dining table under the trees.

“So, why is this here?” Stone asked. He waved his hand to indicate the general area.

“It’s a remnant of the original Witt estate,” Jason said. It was the first time that he had acknowledged the older man’s existence. “That’s why the folly and the fountain. That street was the original drive. And then the other arm of the angle was the drive to Cerridwen’s house. The connecting piece that makes it a full circle wasn’t put in till Teddy’s house was built. When Marshall Witt sold some of the land to recoup his stock losses, he kept title to this piece.”

“Who owns it now? It’s a prime piece of real estate, if an awkward shape.” Stone looked around the park like slice of land.

“The tree owns it.” Jason smiled for the first time that day.

Stone blinked. “I’m sorry, I have to have misheard that. Did you say the tree owns it?”

“Yeah.” Jason shrugged. “It’s a little embarrassing. Marshall Witt left the tree and the land it stands on to the tree. And the city just went with it.”

“But why?” Gerry said.

“Who knows what deviance lurks in the heart of Edwardian millionaires,” Fred opined.

“He did not want the tree disturbed,” Joan interjected.

“The tree?” The question came from Thomas and Stone at the same time.

“The oak.” Jason pointed to the towering specimen that dominated the other end of the court. It had to be over a hundred and fifty feet tall. Its spreading branches shaded the entire grassy clearing and its massive trunk was more than twenty feet around. Cerridwen knew this for a fact, being both curious and in possession of a long measuring tape.

"The tree is why this place is called Green Man Court," Jason added.

"Because of the tree?" Stone asked.

"Because of the faces." Jason stood up and gestured for them to follow him. When they got closer, what had looked like rough texture from a distance was really a face carved into the bark. A grinning face with oak leaves for a mustache. And, further up, another with wings and antlers sprouting from his head. Above that a broad leaf, the veins forming eyes and a sensuous mouth.

"There are more than a hundred of them all over the tree. No one is sure who carved them. I think it had to be more than one person. The styles are all different. And some are obviously older than others," Jason said.

Stone moved closer. "Do they go all the way up?" he asked.

"As high as I've gone," Gerry said from behind them. "But that's only about fifteen or twenty feet."

"You should not have gone even that high," Joan reprimanded him.

"Here we go," Jason mumbled under his breath, just loud enough for Thomas to hear.

"The Green Man is the home of an ancient spirit. You might disturb her if you climb the tree," Joan said.

"Why would a spirit live here of all places?" Fred eyed the tree with distrust.

Joan was more than happy to elaborate. "This tree is all that is left of the forest that used to cover these hills. A dryad protected that forest. She sleeps in this tree. We must treat her with respect." Joan patted the tree affectionately. "And climbing her tree would certainly disturb her."

"She doesn't seem to have done a very good job," Gerry said under his breath, looking around at where the forest wasn't.

"I have two questions," Fred said. "One, why would climbing it bother her more than having things carved into her tree?"

Joan had an answer ready. "The faces are in her honor. They are a sign of reverence."

"And two, who pays the tree's property tax?"

"At 400 years old, Mr. Green Man is a senior citizen and has no income. So his taxes are waived," Jason answered with a straight face.

"So, if the spirit is female, how come everyone refers to the tree as male?" Thomas asked as they moved back towards the picnic.

"Oh, well, there is a simple answer for that. I have no idea," Jason said.

Over lunch Joan reminded everyone of her "come as a past life" Halloween party, an annual event. This sparked a rambling conversation that bounced back and forth between past life regression and costume ideas. Eventually the party broke into two parts: Teddy, the Sands sisters, and Joan telling Michael Stone about people they had known and he might like to write about, and the boys throwing a ball around while Cerridwen tried to figure out how soon she could sneak back to the house and kill Norland's sister.

Jason Witt, determined to hold his own against the younger men, flung the ball as far and as high as he could. It flew through the crisp, blue sky in a perfect arc. It might have gone on forever but for the Green Man. It crashed through the branches and made a deep thumping noise as it sailed into a hollow near the crown of the giant tree. The four of them stared at the tree for a beat of silence. Fred was the first to recover.

"Have I ever mentioned I'm deathly afraid of heights?"

"Coward," accused Gerry.

"Yes, Ginger. That's what I said." They continued to look at the tree. "But I would like my ball back."

"It's a Nerf ball. Get another one," said Thomas said.

"At today's prices?" Fred sounded skeptical. The other three eyed each other.

"My mother would pitch a bitch fit if she caught me in that tree. It's like sacred or something." Jason held up his hands and took a big step backwards.

"Rock, paper, scissors?" Thomas suggested to Gerry.

"Well, you are taller than me," Gerry pointed out.

Thomas sighed and bowed to the inevitable. He went over to the tree and reached up. Flat-footed, he grabbed a branch and hauled himself up.

"See?" Gerry called. "You didn't even have to jump."

"Bite me," Thomas offered in a conversational tone. He had made it about halfway up before the rest of the group noticed his ascent. He distantly heard Joan protest the "molestation" of a sacred tree.

"I do not think that word means what she thinks it means," he mused as he hauled himself higher. "I'm just trying not to reenact Pooh and the honey tree." He studied his next move. "In the words of a great bear, 'Oh help.'" He managed the last ten feet with sheer determination, cursing Fred and Nerf all the way.

Thomas braced his feet on a branch below the hollow and, looping his arm over a branch above his head, he eased around the trunk to look into the opening. He immediately wished he hadn't. A beam of late afternoon sun lit up the opening. It lent a golden halo to the Nerf football as it lay cradled in the long-fingered hand of a skeleton. It had its knees pulled up and head twisted to look toward him, with one arm pinned behind the ribcage and the other out flung as if offering him the ball.

He nearly took a step backwards. He had bent over to look in the opening, and having his weight so far forward saved him. He clutched at the branch above him and threw his free hand out to slap against the trunk. After a moment of stark terror, Thomas went down the same way he had come up, only much faster. He did not take the care he had on his way up and his hands and his jeans paid the price. He reached the bottom in a rush of speed and a shower of yellow leaves. Joan was ready to take him to task. He ignored her with skill honed by hours of child wrangling.

"You seem to have misplaced my ball," Fred pointed out.

"Do you have your phone on you?" Thomas asked without preamble.

"No, left it at the house," Fred said.

Gerry just shook his head. Joan drew breath for another attempt to read him the riot act.

Thomas reached past her as Cerridwen offered her phone. He turned his back as he scrolled through numbers until he found Jane's.

Joan threw her hands in the air and stomped away. Jason watched his mother leave then turned to Gerry. "Allow me to paraphrase. 'Sacred tree, blah, blah, and blah.'"

"Interesting. History blah blah?" said Gerry said.

"Where is my ball? And why is he making a phone call?" Fred said to no one in particular.

"Your ball is still in the tree," Thomas answered. Joan was sulking at the other end of the angle, but those near him had grown silent. With a thoughtful look in their direction, Ruby moved closer. Thomas turned away again as Jane picked up.

"Cerridwen?" she asked.

"No, it's Thomas."

"Is she OK?"

"She's fine. But someone else isn't. There is a body in the Green Man. Scratch that," he corrected himself. "There is what's left of a body in the Green Man."

There was a single startled exclamation behind him, then if anything, the silence grew more intense as his listeners drew closer.

"What, just hanging in the branches?"

"No, in a hollow about forty feet up. It's been there for a while by the looks of it."

"Interesting note in history awhile? Or this is now going to become my problem awhile?" asked Jane.

"I couldn't tell you. But either way, I'm betting whoever it was didn't get up there without help."

"I'm already on my way."

"What should I do with everybody in the meantime?"

"Everybody?"

"Ruby was having a picnic. There are about ten people out here, give or take."

"Not counting the one up the tree." Jane sighed. "Round them up and take them to Random House. I'll be there in twenty."

Chapter 8

Thomas had gotten everyone across the street and into the house with the practiced cat herding skill of an elementary school music teacher. They had accepted the news of a corpse and a change of location with varying degrees of resignation.

Michael Stone and Jason Witt had found a common bond in the kitchen. Teddy had retired to one end of the library with his grandfather's hand painted illustrated Kama Sutra. At the other end of the library, Joan was having some kind of fit of vapors. Pearl and Ruby hovered around her, remarking alternately that this was so unlike her, and how sensitive poor Joan had always been.

Cerridwen had snuck off to a quiet corner to see if she could do in Norland's sister before the cops showed up. The boys had retreated to the front parlor which was crammed with musical instruments. As she worked, she could faintly hear what sounded like White Snake's greatest hits for piano. Thankfully Joan's wails had subsided into a weepy discontent.

After deep thought, Cerridwen decided that drowning offered the most opportunity for Hal to screw up and therefore get caught. He was holding Ann under water, waiting for the bubbles to stop rising, when Jane arrived.

"I'm taking over Teddy's back parlor for the next few hours. We'll take a statement from everyone, but it shouldn't take long since Thomas is the only one who saw anything."

"We?" Cerridwen asked absently. Ann had stopped struggling and it seemed time for Hal to leave her face down in the pool and let nature take its course.

"They've given me a partner. Jesús Esposito. Young, but bright. I don't know how much help all this will be. Whatever happened took place years ago."

"My guess is that it happened about fifty years ago, give or take." How long would it take for Ann's bruises to show up?

"You think you know who it is?" Jane eyed her thoughtfully.

"I think it's Mary Paul. She was one of Witt's hangers-on back in the 60s. Anyway, it's a theory. How does drowning affect lividity?"

"No idea. You're probably right. You usually are. Drives me nuts, by the way." Jane had no problem having more than one conversation at once. It was one of the things that made her the perfect roommate. The gun kind of helped, too.

"Not always. I just go with what would make the best plot. And sometimes real-life criminals turn out to be just as devious as me. Just not all the time." She shrugged.

"So half of this group wouldn't even have been born yet."

"And the other half would have been very much alive and in the thick of all the drama." Cerridwen would have elaborated, but a tidy combination of suit and muscle appeared in the doorway.

"It took me ten minutes to find you," the suit said to Jane. "I've been wandering from room to room while more and more people couldn't tell me where you were. This place is huge. Finally got some old guy with antique porn to point me in the right direction."

"Is the medical examiner here yet?" Jane asked.

"A bit ago. He took one look at that tree and the ladder and demanded a cherry picker. He's making noises about scaffolding."

“I need to know gender and how long it’s been in the tree.”

“You got a lead?” The suit went on alert. He reminded Cerridwen of a retriever on point.

“A suggestion. I need to know how probable it is,” Jane said. Cerridwen mumbled under her breath, but not low enough to slip past Jane’s keen ears. “I know your thoughts. But just because it makes the best story doesn’t mean it’s what happened.”

“But it should,” Cerridwen told the now empty room. With a sigh she went back to the world where her word was law.

* * * *

Jane worked her way through the group with cool efficiency. The process was sped up by the fact that most of the group hadn’t even been aware that Thomas was up the tree.

Joan had put forward the theory that the skeleton belonged to an ancient tribute to the tree spirit and should not be disturbed. She had responded to the outright refusal to accept her pronouncement with sulky defiance. Her son had borne her off, a little dazed by the change in his mother.

While Cerridwen waited her turn to recount what she had and hadn’t seen, she considered the pros and cons of Hal’s mother-in-law breaking her neck.

When Detective Esposito escorted Teddy out of the room, he was startled to see her lying with her head resting on the black and white tiled circles of the entry floor and her legs trailing up the staircase at an awkward angle.

“If you don’t mind my asking, what are you doing?” His tone implied only mild curiosity.

“Pretending to break my neck,” she answered reasonably.

“Oh, well, you’re doing it wrong.”

“Am I?” she asked with interest. “Do tell.” She threw out an arm for the notebook on the floor beside her.

“You’d be more crumpled,” Jesús explained. “More like in a heap then laid out like that. Pretty much everything would be at an unnatural angle. Most people who break their neck on a flight of stairs look a lot like a pile of laundry."

"Good to know. Maybe should she just fake break her neck." Cerridwen, still upside down, braced the notebook against her knee and scribbled furiously. "Oh! Hey, maybe it's a trap! That could work. I have to rewrite chapter six though."

The detective turned to look towards the front of the house. "What is that sound?" he asked.

Cerridwen paused to listen. "'Smooth Criminal' on violin and antique piano."

"Really?"

"Yeah, apparently you can play pretty much anything on any instrument you want. You haven't lived till you've heard Nine Inch Nails' 'Closer' played on an oboe."

"Really!?"

"No, I'm kidding. Maybe. Well, look at that! Hal's mother-in-law just became the hero. Crap rewrites. Oh, I'm sorry, did you want something?"

"Jane wants to speak to you."

"Right. My turn." Cerridwen set the notebook on the stairs and started to the door of the living room. Having second thoughts, she went back and picked up the notebook. Having third thoughts, she set it on the console table and then decided to take it with her after all, only to discover somewhere between the stairs and the coffee table she had lost her pen. Again.

Jane motioned her to sit on the couch and offered her a pen. In the year since she moved in, she had taken to buying pens in bulk and just periodically handing one to Cerridwen. "So, start at the beginning. Why were you all out there to begin with?"

"Ruby and Thomas used lunch to lure me out of the house. They're worried about me or something." She couldn't quite keep the sulky tone out of her voice.

"We're all worried about you. You still have a concussion."

"I still have a deadline. And it's been a week. Besides, how much sleep do I really need?" As soon as the words left her mouth, she knew she had made a mistake.

"You are supposed to rest. You are still recovering from head trauma. As soon as we're done here, you are going to bed."

Cerridwen knew better than to argue with that calm, flat tone. Better people than her had tried and failed.

Jane switched gears effortlessly. "You're having a picnic and the guys are throwing the ball. What happened next?"

"I wasn't actually paying attention. Joan had started to pontificate about Daddy's legacy to her new friend and I was wondering how soon I could get back to work."

"So what was the first thing you did notice?"

"Joan broke off her monologue to yell at the boys for climbing the tree. Something about the tree being sacred. We all pretty much wrote it off as-raised-by-the-tea-prophet nonsense. By that time, Thomas was about thirty feet up and ignored her. Fred said the tree could play fair or get its own ball and Joan fumed at them for a bit and then settled down. Her pet biographer managed to smooth her ruffled feathers." She was trying to pay attention to Jane, but she was tired and wanted to finish Ann off before the end of the day. "You couldn't really see what was going on up there. There's still a lot of leaves, and he was a few stories up by that point."

"And when he came down?" Jane asked. She reached over and took the pen back. It was then that Cerridwen realized she had been clicking it incessantly. "How did people react when he came back down?"

"Joan tried to chide him again. I've never actually used that word in conversation before, but it seems to fit."

"How did he answer her?"

"He didn't. He didn't even tell us what was going on at first. The first thing he did was ask for a phone. He called you, asked you what to do, and then rounded us all up." Cerridwen unsuccessfully smothered a yawn.

Just then, a man in a bunny costume entered the room. The costume was oddly lacking in ears. On closer inspection, it turned out to be some sort of overall.

"Well, it's certainly not a tree spirit," he informed them without preamble. "Most definitely human. And a modern one at that."

"You can tell that from the skeleton?" asked Jane.

"Well, with close study certainly," the man in the non-bunny suit answered. "But for now I'm basing the assumption on the fact that ancient tree spirits don't use zippers."

"Plastic or metal?" Cerridwen asked.

"Plastic."

"Did it have a placket or was it an invisible zipper?"

"There really isn't enough fabric left to tell. It's very moist on the inside of a tree. And then there are bugs."

"Down the center of the back?"

"Most likely since it was pinned between the spine and the inside of the tree."

"The earliest you would see that in a dress was the 1960s," Cerridwen pointed out. "I told you so," she mouthed at Jane.

Jane made a face at her. "Take your notebook and your imaginary friends and go to bed," she said sternly.

Cerridwen left reluctantly. But she was now ninety percent sure it was Mary Paul in that tree. She smothered another yawn and went upstairs to colonize Gerry's bedroom not because she was tired she told herself, but because Jane would find out if she didn't. She spent the few minutes before sleep hit wondering why you would go to all the bother of stuffing Mary Paul in a tree. It seemed like a lot of effort. And how did you pull off that kind of thing without someone seeing?

* * * *

Thomas ushered the last of the ill-fated picnickers out of the house. No, not the last. Fred and Ginger were still in the house. He paused to consider when he had picked up Teddy's habit of referring to Fred and Gerry as the song and dance team. And Teddy was still lurking in the library. Well, now it was family, in a weird extended kind of way. He went into the living room. "Is Christ staying for dinner?" he asked.

Jane stared at him, confused.

"It's Jesús," her partner corrected him.

"Sorry, it's been a long day. Are you staying for dinner?"

"I might as well." He looked to Jane for confirmation.

"So, you two, Gerry, Fred, Teddy. That's five. Me and Cerridwen, that's seven. Chinese or pizza? Cause I am not cooking for that many people on this short a notice."

"Make it China Garden and I'll chip in," Jane told him. "Are you keeping Cerridwen over night?"

"Are you working tonight?"

"Yeah."

"Then she's staying."

Her partner had been listening to the exchange with a frown. "You're asking a guy you've known all of a week to co-op your roommate?"

Jane shook her head. "I know him well enough. Her cousin and her great uncle are here as well. In a fair fight my money would be on Teddy, except he doesn't fight fair. And I don't care to leave my concussed roommate alone with that out there." She gestured in the direction of the Green Man and its grisly contents.

"It's been there for years," Jesús pointed out.

"These houses haven't changed hands in over a century. There is a better than even chance that whoever put her there is still here," she answered.

"And a million years old," Jesús muttered.

"Remembering the 60s does not make you a million years old," Jane said a little tartly.

"Felix's house changed hands," Thomas corrected her. "He said something about buying it the first time he hit the bestseller list."

"Who did he buy it from?" Jane made a note.

"Original owner's grandchildren, I think. I wasn't paying attention. It was only in passing. And there is the tiny fact that we still don't know who wandered into the house at will and tried to bash Cerridwen's head in," Thomas pointed out.

"Did Cerridwen go to bed?"

"After I took away anything she could write with. I'll let her have her computer back after dinner. She won't eat otherwise." Thomas went to call in the order. Jesús followed him out into the hall. He was accompanied by the sound of "Bad Boys" by Inner Circle. Thomas thought it was totally appropriate, especially since the rhythm worked with Esposito's swagger.

"Mind if I ask you something?"

"Go for it. People have been asking all day."

"You and Miss Evan-Jones, is it serious?"

"At this point, about as serious as a heart attack."

The detective was nonplussed for a moment. "So, if someone else expressed an interest?"

"Dude, I'm flattered, but you're not really my type."

"I was referring to Miss Evan-Jones."

"Oh, well, in that case, I would stab you in the eye," Thomas informed him cheerfully

"Understood." He retreated to the living room.

Thomas watched him go. "Damn right," he muttered to himself. "The nerve of that guy. And me practically imaginarily engaged." He resolved to make sure that "Jesus" didn't get any egg rolls.

Chapter 9

Thomas stuck his head in the door of the library to tell Cerridwen that they were out of food. “Except for tortillas and a jar of peanut butter, and that way lies madness.”

“I suppose someone will have to go to the grocery store,” she responded absently.

“I was planning on it, but I don’t think I should leave you unsupervised.”

“I’ve survived unsupervised before,” she pointed out. “If memory serves, I am older than you.”

“Age has nothing to do with maturity. You’re still having dizzy spells from the concussion. And you forget to eat.”

“Well, the last part is hardly relevant since there is no food in the house anyway. If you were drowned in the bathtub you would probably have bath salts in your lungs, right? Or maybe bath oils. Yes, I think you would definitely have jasmine oil in your lungs.”

For some reason this seem to firm his resolve. “I’m going to go find someone to babysit you,” Thomas told her.

"And I am going back to ignoring you," Cerridwen answered cheerfully.

Fred and Gerry had both gone to work. Pearl told him she was in the middle of yet another sex scene and he would have to call back after her characters broke up for the second time. Ruby had a Garden Club meeting to attend.

"The mind boggles. I would not have thought gardening was your thing," Thomas said to her.

"Well, there is a bit of gardening," Ruby said. "But truthfully it's really an excuse to wear huge hats and drink rum."

Felix said, "I would love to help, but it would be a little difficult as I am still in Portland at a book signing. Cerridwen will probably be fine on her own. What are the chances of her getting coshed on the head twice in one week?"

"That's what I thought before I realized you people left dead bodies lying around."

"What bodies? Where?"

"Oh, never mind," Thomas snapped and hung up.

In the end, he had to settle for Teddy. He clung to the theory that they would watch each other so that neither could get into too much trouble. It was not until after he had left that they both agreed that this was a huge mistake on his part.

"So, have they decided who that person in the tree was?" Teddy asked as he settled in.

"They're still working on it. I think it was Mary Paul."

"That would explain why Joan was so upset," Teddy suggested.

"It would only explain it if she knew it was Mary. And how could she when none of us knew it was there?" Cerridwen pointed out.

"She's usually so levelheaded. I wondered if she hadn't had some of Daddy's tea that morning."

"So whatever drug he was using was in the tea?" The phrase puzzled her.

"Well, why did you think he was called the tea prophet?"

"Because of his father's tea fortune." She began to suspect that maybe that wasn't the reason.

"Well, yes, his father did make a ridiculous amount of money importing tea. But that was not the tea that gave Thaddeus his nickname. Before he went into his trance and had his visions, he drank an herbal tea. I suspect that they were not herbs in the strictest sense of the word."

"Hallucinogenic?" Cerridwen was intrigued. "Any idea which one?"

"Couldn't tell you. Not really my bag." Teddy shrugged. "Always thought his parents kind of set him up for it. Who names their child Thaddeus?"

Cerridwen went to the bookshelf and hauled down a big book. It hadn't taken her any time to find the book she wanted. She was as familiar with Teddy's library as her own. "What kind of visions?" she asked as she flipped pages.

"Conversations with his spirit guides, mostly. Sounded like imaginary friends to me. And some ranting about everything having a glowing aura." Teddy narrowed his eyes in an effort to remember, as if he could see the past better if he squinted.

"That sounds familiar. Hang on a second." She flipped farther into the book and then back. "I can't remember if it's under D or J. Ah, here it is. Any myoclonic movements?"

"Say what now?" Teddy frowned at her.

"Twitching," she clarified.

"Yes, bit of that. And an odd insistence on a post ritual cleansing bath. Crazy about his baths, I seem to remember."

"Hot or cold?" she asked, running her finger down the page.

"Cold most certainly. Remember thinking it was strange at the time. Used to get red all over." Teddy scratched his chin thoughtfully.

"Got it. Thaddeus Witt was opening his mind with datura."

"Da- what?"

"Jimsonweed. Most likely the seeds. It might have had other things in it. But from what you describe, it would seem to be the main ingredient."

Cerridwen turned the book so he could see the illustration.

"Not one I ever tried. I seem to remember opium was nice. But most drugs seem vastly overrated. What I don't understand about all this business is why stuff her in the tree in the first place. Regardless of who it is, it seems a highly inefficient way to get rid of a body."

"It kept the body hidden for what—fifty-plus years," said Cerridwen said. She stuffed the book on poisonous plants back on to the shelf.

"And you have to wonder," Teddy looked towards the front of the house in the direction of the giant oak. "How they got it up there."

They eyed each other, gauging each other's intent.

"Well, to start with, we need a tree." Cerridwen was thoughtful. After a moment of contemplation, they both rushed for the door. Teddy could move as fast as a man half his age. Speeding down the front steps, they fetched up on the sidewalk to find the grassy expanse across the street festooned with yellow tape. Two police officers eyed them with distrust from the other side of the barrier. People in overalls milled around doing inexplicable things with expensive pieces of equipment.

"They do not look inclined to share," Teddy observed.

Cerridwen surveyed the front garden. "The crab apple will have to do."

"It's not nearly high enough." He eyed the tree in question.

"Make do and mend," she told him.

"That makes no sense."

"Do you really want to climb that high?"

"I had assumed that you would do the climbing." Teddy batted his eyes at her. "Me being so old and frail, you know."

She wrinkled her nose at him. "So, now we need a body. And I'm guessing some rope."

"How big a body?" Teddy was always practical.

It was one of the things she loved about him. She took her phone and called Jane. "So how big was the corpse in the tree? Back when it was fresh, I mean."

"And good morning to you, too," answered Jane answered. "And why do you want to know?"

Curse Jane and her untrusting nature. "Morbid curiosity?" Cerridwen offered.

"Oh, good one. She'll totally buy that," Teddy whispered loudly. She hushed him.

"Is that Teddy? What are the two of you up to?" Jane demanded.

"Absolutely nothing illegal," Cerridwen said brightly. Teddy gave her a thumbs up. She could hear voices in the background and what might have been Jane hitting her head against the desk.

"Keep it that way and I'll give you her vital statistics."

"So, it was female?" She gave a crow of triumph. Jane sighed loudly. "Sorry, you were saying?"

"Female, Five foot six, 120 pounds. Give or take."

"Do you know who she is yet?"

"Still waiting on dental records. Please don't do anything that means I have to bail you out," Jane pleaded before she hung up.

"A little smaller and lighter than me. No, Theodore." She anticipated his next question. "You are not hauling me into that tree."

"We could extrapolate. If we reduced the size and weight by the same proportion, the experiment would still render usable results. Or we could pop down to town and see if the hardware store sells crash test dummies. But I think the first option is the better bet." Teddy gazed up at the tree.

And that is why they were hauling a bag of flour into the crab apple when the Hawkner appeared on the sidewalk bellow.

"What are you doing?" she demanded.

"Lowering the tone of the neighborhood. And after we're done, Teddy's going to sunbathe," Cerridwen answered as she swung from a rope thrown over a branch. Teddy wiggled his eyebrows suggestively at Ms. Hawkner, who shuddered elaborately.

Cerridwen ignored them both. The branch was not as high as she would have liked, but it was as high as she had been able to get before the dizziness did her in. She was not recovering from the knock to the head as fast as she would have liked.

"Why on Earth are you trying to haul a bag of flour into a tree? And a 150-year-old crab apple at that. It's practically a historic landmark on its own."

"Yes. But it's *my* historic landmark." Teddy couldn't resist getting a dig in.

"We're trying to discover how the body was placed into that hollow in the oak," Cerridwen told her.

Hawkner pursed her lips in obvious disapproval. "It will turn out to be that Paul woman. And no surprise she came to a bad end."

"Mary?" Teddy thought about that for a moment. "I don't see it. She was a friendly girl, nice to everybody. No reason to bump her off and shove her in a tree. No reason to do that to anybody, really."

"I won't go so far as to say they had reason." Judging by her expression, she would have liked to say just that. "But you can't deny it was a scandal. Living in the house and carrying on with that man."

"I had thought her relationship with Thaddeus was platonic."

"Not Witt," Hawkner snapped. She was clearly irritated by his misunderstanding. "Paul was carrying on under his nose with that hippie boy that called himself a photographer. And both of them living in Whitmore the whole while. William Witt was probably turning in his grave."

That caught Cerridwen attention. "What hippie boy?"

"Thorn something." Hawkner sniffed.

"Thornapple," Teddy supplied. "And stop sniffing at everything, Ann. Your face will stick that way."

"I don't suppose either of you remember his real name?" Cerridwen was curious.

"Of course I don't remember his real name!" Hawkner's tone showed just how silly the whole idea was.

"It sticks in my head that there was something funny about it," Teddy said.

"I couldn't say. I associated with those people as little as possible."

"That means they never asked her to join in any reindeer games. I, on the other hand, have fond memories of several of them. Particularly Lilith. Nice girl, used to wear this flowing skirt and nothing else," Teddy said in a not-so-quiet aside with a dreamy sigh.

Hawkner gave a finale huff of indignation before striding off towards her own house.

"What's got her all worked up? Not that that's an abnormal state for her." Cerridwen gave another tug at the rope and the bag of flour rose another foot.

"She feels ill-used by the world in general and the Witt family in particular. They're cousins of a sort." Teddy shaded his eyes and studied the branch above them.

"I didn't know they were related." The bag rose again, a little less this time since as the bag got higher it got harder to shift.

"Not closely. And not in any way that she or Joan cares to acknowledge. William Witt's younger son inherited the Gate House to the old estate. Not that it's a gate house in the truest sense of the word. The two sons had a falling out over selling parts of the estate. Never spoke to each other again."

"There is a story in that somewhere," Cerridwen said.

"Not an interesting one. It is the Witt's, after all. The younger son had a daughter. An only child, who married a Hawkner. And thus, Ann. I think that's about as high as we'll get it." He pointed to the much-abused bag of flour dangling a few feet above their heads. Cerridwen tied the end of the rope to a wrought iron lawn chair and caught her breath.

"So, is the ill will left over from that disagreement or is there something more?"

"Well, the Hawkners have always felt that the wrong branch of the family inherited the bulk of the estate and the Witt fortune. They felt that Thaddeus' behavior only proved them right. And they weren't shy about saying it, either. And there's Ann, a few years older than Joan, seeing Joan getting everything that she was told should be hers. And, in Ann's opinion, misusing it horribly. It just made her more sour."

"And her scheme to turn anything that holds still long enough into a museum?" Cerridwen hauled herself into the tree. She paused on the first branch to wait for the world to stop spinning. If she ever found out who had hit her, she was going to murder them. Slowly and possibly more than once.

"A lust for power," Teddy suggested. "We all have our little quirks. What did the rope do to the branch?"

Cerridwen examined the limb. "It scraped up the bark. And there are fibers from the rope sticking to the branch. With something heavier and a greater height the damage would have been more."

"What are you doing?" The question was fired from the sidewalk for the second time that day.

"Cheese it. It's the cops," Teddy mumbled out of the side of his mouth. Cerridwen peered down through the fall leaves. Jesús Esposito was visible just the other side of the low garden wall.

"Jane gets a phone call from you and spends the next hour saying, 'No they wouldn't' under her breath. Then the CSI guys across the street call in to say that there's suspicious behavior going on in your front yard. And I get here to find the two of you up a tree. Now, what is going on?"

"Nonsense." Teddy dismissed the question out of hand. "Only one of us is in the tree. And you need to have a word with those boys about sharing. They've been glaring at us judgmentally since we came out here with a rope and a bag of flour."

Esposito sighed and ran his fingers through his hair. Cerridwen had eased her way down by this point.

"I repeat, what were you doing in the tree?"

"We are recreating events," Teddy said loftily.

Thomas came up the walk towards them, a grocery bag in either hand. He took in the scene with one glance and then seemed to ignore it.

"I brought home lunch." He held one of the bags out. "And paper plates so that no one has to do dishes."

"How very thoughtful." Cerridwen smiled at him.

"Aren't you going to ask them what they've been up to?" Jesús asked.

"Well, it's rather obvious what they're up to if you take the time to look," he pointed out in a mild tone.

"And that doesn't bother you?"

"If shoving imaginary murder victims into trees bothers you, then Cerridwen is not the girl for you." Thomas shrugged. "Honestly, I never get tired of watching her act out a murder. Are you staying for lunch? We're having tacos."

Chapter 10

The little group congregated in the kitchen. Thomas delegated slicing and grating, then browned hamburger. Jesús stood in the doorway, watching them. He tried to project disapproval, but the shot went wide and landed somewhere between bewilderment and amusement.

"Doesn't it bother any of you that you've known each other all of a week and you're practically living in each other's pockets?" he said.

"Nonsense," Teddy responded. "I've known him more than a week. And he pays rent, kind of. He's really my babysitter, but I'm not supposed to know that."

"I was speaking to Miss Evan-Jones," the detective corrected him.

"Well, that hardly makes any more sense. Known her all her life. I was married to her grandmother, after all."

Esposito's pocket rang loudly and he fumbled for his phone. "Yes? No. They've stopped now."

"Hi, Jane," Cerridwen raised her voice. "I know how they got the body in the tree."

He frowned at her, turned away, and covered one ear. "Making tacos. I don't know. Hang on." He turned back. "Are you done terrorizing the neighborhood?"

Cerridwen shrugged.

"For now," Teddy answered.

The detective glared at them, ear still glued to the phone, listening for a moment before he hung up.

"You are to behave yourselves till she gets home." Jesús eyed Thomas. "Try to keep them in line. I would suggest locking them up."

Michael Stone knocked sharply on the open back door. He came to a stop when the detective threw his hands in the air.

"How a body stayed hidden that long in this place, I will never know." Jesús stomped out muttering to himself. "People wandering in and out of each other's houses all the damn time."

"What's wrong with him?" Stone hesitated at the door.

"He's finding the local culture difficult to adjust to." Teddy sucked his fingers and eyed the cheese grater distrustfully.

"Interesting. You feel the neighborhood has its own culture?" Stone was intrigued.

"It's really more of a lifestyle," Thomas offered. "You have to make a conscious effort to give up sanity."

"I don't think Ms. Witt made a decision to be insane. I think she is just finding the situation a little stressful emotionally."

"Oh," Thomas said. "Were we talking about Ms. Witt?"

"No. It's just where my mind is at the moment. I don't understand why she is so wrapped up in that tree spirit story. It's a fairy tale."

"No one but Joan seems to pay it much attention." Cerridwen shrugged. "She's older than me. I wasn't here all the time as a kid. I was traveling a lot with Mom or I was at the theater with Dad. And when I was here I had two and a half acres of garden to ramble all over.

I never really spent that much time on the Angle till I was older. And by then tree climbing had lost its charm. It's hard on the wardrobe."

"And you?" Stone turned to Teddy.

"I was all over that tree as a boy. All over the neighborhood, really. But in my day there was no talk of tree spirits. No dead body either, if they're right about the time frame."

"So the myth of the tree spirit is fairly recent?"

Cerridwen thought about it for a moment. "I don't think I've ever heard anyone but Joan talk about it. I wonder where she picked it up. Or, more importantly, when." She chewed her lip.

"What are you thinking?" Thomas set the tray of tacos on the table and pulled out the chair next to her.

"If I was writing this. The spirit story and the murder would have happened at the same time. Joan would have been ten or eleven. I would have used the kid to spread the story in a way that couldn't be traced to me. It would keep people away from the tree. I wonder if they meant to leave the body there all this time or if they had plans to move it at some point. But then, I have a dirty mind."

"I prefer to think you have an agile mind," Thomas commented.

"Your grandmother had an agile mind." Teddy sighed into the sour cream. "God, what a woman. Best six months of my life married to her."

Thomas was lost in contemplation of women with agile minds.

Stone fastened on Cerridwen's theory. "You think the murderer fed her the story as a blind?"

"Can't say, I wasn't there. But it would make a good story. And I would be interested in just where she got the idea that the spirit in the Green Man was a woman."

"I noticed that, too." Stone nodded. "It's an interesting detail." He helped himself to a taco. This did not sit well with Thomas. Cerridwen needed to eat, and feeding Teddy had become more or less routine. This guy had dug in without even the formality of inviting himself to lunch. His welcome was not a foregone conclusion. It wasn't like he was Ruby and Pearl or even Felix. He watched a second taco make the trip to Stone's mouth.

"Was there a reason you dropped by? Something you needed?" He intentionally dropped his already deep voice another fraction of an octave. Just enough to make the other man uneasy. Stone swallowed hastily and nearly choked on crispy taco shell.

"I wanted to ask about sources. The word is that your grandmother kept journals. Some of them might coincide with some interesting events in Witt's life. I would like to use them as a secondary source." Stone addressed Cerridwen, but he watched Thomas nervously. Teddy was engrossed in his tacos. Thomas was the only one looking at Cerridwen. Only he saw the flick of the eyebrow and ever so slight tightening of the mouth.

"I wouldn't think they would be of much help. She and Witt didn't move in the same circles. They ignored each other for the most part. And she did a lot of filming on location. She wasn't here a lot during the high point of his career."

"Any little bit would help." Stone persisted. "Another viewpoint would be helpful."

"They belong to the estate. It's in trust. So any request like that would have to go through the trustees. And it's not likely to a be a yes. She was very explicit in her instructions regarding her personal effects." She did not elaborate on those instructions or how to contact the trustees. If he had done his research he would know that Teddy and Ruby were the people he needed to talk to. But she saw no reason to make him a present of the information. In any case, the answer would be no.

"I am intrigued by the connection between Witt and Paul." There was hesitation over the second name. Did he have difficulty remembering it? "So much is known about Witt. He was a very prolific author. But there seems to be so little record of Mary Paul. And so much has already been written about him. This would be a new angle. A new lens brought to bear, so to speak."

"And it would be great publicity." Cerridwen's voice was sugar sweet. Thomas could tell that it was meant as a dig. But Stone just smiled.

“Well, murder sells. But I don’t have to tell you that, do I?”

Thomas cleared the table. It would be better to get Stone out of here before Cerridwen's temper got the upper hand. Though, watching her slaughter the man with words had a certain appeal.

Teddy slammed his hand down on the table. “That’s why it was funny.”

“What was funny?” Stone was at sea.

Thomas waited patiently for the conversation to swing back. Teddy usually made sense if you gave him enough time.

“Thornapple. His last name was Thorn. That’s why they all thought it was so clever. It was some sort of play on his last name.” Teddy was pleased he remembered.

“It wasn’t just a play on his name. Thorn-apple is one of the folk names of datura. They were making fun of Witt at the same time.”

“It’s a common enough name, Thorn.” Stone was less than impressed. “I don’t see how it will do you much good without a first name.”

“Even with that it would hard to find someone after all this time. But it might be worth it to see what he knew,” Cerridwen mused.

Teddy shook his head. “There were so many people in and out of that place. It was an ant hill. I don’t know how you would be able to separate the truth at this late date.”

“You said earlier he was a photographer?”

“He called himself a photographer, but every kid with a camera thought they were a photographer. There were probably an even dozen people over there taking pictures at any given time. I doubt he had credentials any more impressive than a driver's license.” Teddy shook his head. “I’m afraid Thorn would be hard to find.”

“How about any of the others?” Stone pressed.

“I didn’t know any of them well. I can give you first names or nicknames but no real information. There was Thorn, and Lilith that I told you about,” Teddy said to Cerridwen, waving his hands suggestive of ample curves when he said Lilith. “There was that Jewish princess that called herself Mirra, and some boy they all called Toad. I have no idea why. There were dozens more that I can't even put a nickname to. I don't know anything that could help you find them. I am a veritable dead end."

Cerridwen returned to Witt's End and spent a productive afternoon tightening her plot. She was quite happy with the way the rewrite on chapter ten and eleven pulled the whole thing together. It had the added benefit of making what she thought was a mistake in the second chapter look like a brilliant plot twist.

She retreated to the little room that a century ago had been referred to as the private parlor. She had made only small changes, adding the slate blue sofa from her old apartment and a modest flat screen. She was using an eighteenth century marquetry lady's table as an end table. There were people who would have had a heart attack over this, but she always used a coaster on the fragile wood. And she followed her great grandmother's philosophy that beautiful things should be used.

Others had seen the house and its contents as an elaborate bribe to the beautiful French opera singer, luring her away from the bright lights of Paris. The exquisite diva had seen at as more of a refuge. "When beautiful things are put under glass they die. When they are used for their intended purpose, then they have life. I understand this. I have escaped from under the glass. In my home we are allowed to breathe," she had written in her diary.

What was it like to feel trapped under glass? It was something to think about over a glass of wine and a B movie. That was what Cerridwen was doing when Jane came home.

"I think the body was hauled up the tree by a rope thrown over a high branch. It would take a bit of strength, but it can be done. If you find the right branch you should able to find the scar the friction from the rope left," she told Jane.

"You mean you don't have the rope in question neatly tied around the murderer?" Jane was amused.

"Not yet. But I can tell you it was probably nylon. It was the most readily available, massed produced and durable. The kind of thing that you could have found lying around in the garden. At least three of the houses in Green Man Court had full time gardeners then." She had run through her store of knowledge on the subject. And having solved that part of the puzzle, Cerridwen was ready to move on.

"How did they get the body from the end of the rope to the inside of the tree?"

"I still haven't worked that part out yet. At least not how to do it with just one person," she admitted. She offered Jane, who was distracted, a glass of wine.

"You've been here all day?"

"I haven't left the court all day. But I've been at Teddy's, in a tree, or the back of the house for most of it."

"So" Jane studied her glass. "You haven't noticed anyone wandering about with a can of spray paint?"

Cerridwen tore her attention away from the aliens on the screen. Well, she thought they were meant to be aliens. They might have been giant rubber broccoli, it was hard to tell.

"Spray paint?"

Jane nodded and motioned toward the front of the house. Kimono flapping, slippers slapping Cerridwen went down the hall and out the front door, Jane close behind her.

From the garden gate it was clearly visible—four foot letters in blurry red spray paint sprawled across the cracked and heaving sidewalk across the street "Where Did Mary Go?"

"We're not the only ones that think that body is Mary Paul," said Cerridwen.

Jane spent an hour or so trying to figure out when the slogan had appeared. The two patrolmen had left late that afternoon, they and the ME convinced they had gathered what little evidence there was to find after five decades. So the best anyone could offer was the window between five and eight p.m. No one had seen or heard anything, and no one was missing a can of red spray paint.

There was a brief flurry of activity with a patrol car and a photographer. Cerridwen withdrew to her bedroom with her bottle of wine. It seemed to have lost more than half its contents along the way.

That might have explained the pleasant blur her thoughts had acquired. She tried to remember something, but she could not drag it into focus.

She studied the floor to ceiling shelves that covered the wall between the bedroom and the sinfully large closet. Something about books, she was almost certain. It was probably important was her last thought as she curled up and went to sleep.

Chapter 11

At three a.m., Cerridwen was awake. She fumbled for the gilt and crystal lamp, nearly knocking it off the bedside table. Everyone wanted the same thing, she thought. Stone was looking for it. Hawkner wanted it as well, while Joan went slightly green anytime someone mentioned it. The burglar was probably looking for it, too. The weird part was that it took her so long to think of it. It all came down to books.

She was a writer and a reader, descended from a long line of readers. A few of them with money to burn. There was a room downstairs called the library, but it was more of a suggestion really. The more impressive volumes in great grandfather's collection were stored there, along with the books that no one really used or wanted. But to be honest the entire house was a library with books in every nook and cranny, with the possible exception of the ballroom.

The books most important to her were on the shelves in her bedroom. That's where she found what so many people were looking for. On the bottom shelf, a rainbow of mismatched books each neatly stamped with the year—Constance Frey's journals. Cerridwen crouched on the floor and ran her fingers down the spines till she found 1965.

That summer Mary Paul vanished from the face of the Earth. More than one person seemed to think that Grandma Constance knew something. The only way to find out was to read the journal. And she would be damned if anyone but her read them. The trust established by her grandmother's will all but said she would go straight to hell if these volumes ever saw the light of day. And she believed it. Grandma Constance was perfectly capable of reaching from beyond the grave. She was that kind of woman.

Cerridwen skimmed rapidly looking for any mention of Mary. She found the first one in early March.

"By sheer coincidence my friend Mary has come to town. We met years ago on the club circuit before I started in films. She has decided that life as a magicians' assistant holds few prospects for a secure future. Past a certain age it becomes more difficult to fold one's self into a tiny box. She has returned to her former career of bookkeeper.

"Witt has advertised for an estate accountant. He says between managing his 'community of souls' and pursuing his 'vision' he simply hasn't the time to keep track of the money flowing in and out of Whitmore. I think he's just incapable of higher math. Mary excels at it. She is happy to have a less physically demanding job and I am overjoyed to have her so near."

All these years and many retelling of her story and Cerridwen had never heard the reason for Mary being here. It was Mary's story and somehow Mary never rated top billing. Most versions assumed that Mary was Witt's something on the side. None of them mentioned that she was his employee. It had never been given as her real reason for being at Whitmore. Cerridwen wondered how that particular fact had fallen by the wayside.

She got off the floor and crawled back into bed taking the little volume with her. For a few months Mary wasn't mentioned except in passing. It wasn't until the end of May that there was an entry with any real information.

"Mary has become increasingly worried about where the money is going. She has plenty of questions and as yet no answers. In her careful estimation, Witt is bringing in nearly twice as much money as what is accounted for in the estate's books.

"Tensions are high at Whitmore and I fear for her safety. So many people jockeying for position and a piece of a very big pie. How long before someone decides she is in the way?

"The atmosphere in Witt's Community of souls is growing more inhospitable. I have given her a key to the conservatory door. This offers her a retreat even when I am away from home. She can take the path through the back garden and no one needs to know where she's gone."

Her Grandmother's words were an eerie echo of the graffiti that marked the present day Victoria. Five decades later, Cerridwen needed very much to know where Mary had gone. She set the book on the table and tried to sleep.

After an hour of this she gave up and got out of bed, the journal tucked under her arm. She tiptoed past Jane's door. Jane always slept with the door open.

Downstairs, she put the kettle on the range and hunted for munchies while the water heated. Cerridwen liked her tea dark and rich, so she had plenty of time to flip through the pages as the tea steeped. She was well into the month of July, nearly to August, before she found what she was looking for.

"…I fly to El Salvador next week to film the jungle scenes. It is a good role, a strong story, and a chance to work with my favorite director.

"But it leaves Mary in the lurch. Further investigation has only deepened her suspicions rather than lay them to rest. Money is coming in both from Witt's family investments and the sale of his books. I use the word book loosely in this case. Ramblings might be a better word.

"He also pulls in a fair amount through speaking engagements and something he calls 'gatherings.' I have no idea what he means by that, and I have no wish to. A bit missing here, a tad skimmed there. Over the past year quite a bit of money has gone unaccounted for. Mary is trying to figure out where it's going. Is it one mastermind or is it the combined efforts of multiple people thinking that no one will miss just a little? I return in two weeks. I hope things do not come to a head till I get back."

Cerridwen started to make notes. She needed to find out exactly when Mary Paul had disappeared. She needed to know when she was first reported missing and who had made the report. Chances were that body in the tree was Mary. She had not got up there by herself. It was highly unlikely, given the evidence, that she had died of natural causes.

Indisputable facts stared her in the face. At least one person had reason to want Mary dead. Mary had a key to Witt's End. That key was now unaccounted for. Someone had broken into Witt's End, possibly using that key.

Were Mary's killer and Cerridwen's burglar the same person? How likely was that five decades later? Why wait so long to try to cover their trail? And why, if they were the same person, leave Cerridwen alive?

She flipped through the accounts of filming a low budget sci-fi thriller in an El Salvador jungle, looking for grandmother's return. There, mid-August, a brief account of the flight and then a string of exclamation points.

"Mary is gone! Just gone! No one is able to tell me when or how. None of those unwashed masses can even tell me how long she has been gone. The only certainty is that she did not pack up and take off as they would have me believe. All of her stuff is still there."

Constance Frey was the one to report Mary missing. Her family lived some distance away and had no reason to think she wasn't still at Whitmore. Her fellow residents were oddly uninterested, and by that point she had been missing for a week or more.

Little evidence produced even smaller results. The local authorities had decided that Mary had probably left for greener pastures and the least said, the soonest mended. In the end it had all been swept under the rug with surprisingly little fuss. Constance was distressed but could find no one to take her part. She became convinced that foul play had befallen her friend Mary Paul. She gathered what evidence she could but lacked the resources to do any real work.

There was another entry in September.

"Little Joan has become strangely withdrawn. She is no longer the vibrant child full of energy that she was before I left for El Salvador. Of course, it might be only the onset of puberty. But is it possible that she has witnessed some traumatic event? My questions have been answered with shrugs, sighs, and a long rambling story about a woman who lives inside a tree. If she knows anything about Mary's disappearance, she is unable to communicate it. I may never know what happened to Mary, although I believe she is dead. The trail has gone cold and I have little skill as a detective. All that is left for me is to mourn her loss. I will take what evidence I have and hide it where a lady keeps her secrets.. As a memorial it is the best I can do."

Cerridwen drummed her fingers on the table. Grandma Constance had raised more questions than she had answered. The information in the journal wasn't worth breaking and entering for—not to mention committing assault.

Cerridwen rubbed the back of her head. It was becoming a habit. Where was the key Constance gave to Mary? Is that how the intruder had gotten into the house Tuesday night? What, if anything, had Joan seen? Who had told a little girl an odd story about a woman who lived in a tree?

And above all these questions, where the hell did "a lady keep her secrets?" There was no further mention of Mary or the evidence. The next entry was a brief paragraph in September about buying a table off of Witt. One line caught her eye.

"I was not the first to use it as a hiding place."

If this table was where "a lady kept her secrets," then that narrowed it down. There were only about 200 of them strewn about the place.

Chapter 12

Cerridwen hung around the house in her pajamas waiting for Jane to leave. This meant sitting through a firm but gentle lecture on why people with head trauma should still be asleep at 6 in the morning. *Get brained with a solid silver candle stick and no one ever let you forget it,* Cerridwen fumed.

Jane relented enough before she left to hand Cerridwen a handful of pens and tell her to lose them slowly.

After Jane's departure, Cerridwen waited another hour to make sure that Thomas had left for work just in case he decided he needed to babysit her. Or tie her to a chair to keep her out of trouble. Jane had suggested both as viable options for the care and keeping of wayward roommates.

Once she was sure that she was free of minders, Cerridwen went upstairs to get dressed. In deference to the chilly fall weather, she chose dark pants and a red fitted sweater.

She went into the conservatory. It was a lavish affair of iron and glass, standing almost two stories. Openings in the slate floor accommodated three mature trees. Pausing a moment, she studied the lock. It was original to the house and looked it. The moisture of the conservatory had damaged the finish. There were no clear signs that it had been tampered with, but there wouldn't be if her intruder had had a key.

She went down to the bottom of the garden, taking the back way her grandmother referred to in her journal. It took her rather a long time to hike down the series of steps and paths that wound down to the back gate. She couldn't even see the house from here. The path ran along the stream that marked the boundary between the Green Man Court homes and the parkland below, part of Whitmore's original lavish garden. It edged along her low stone wall for easily a hundred yards.

As she passed the edge of Teddy's property, the stream dropped as the ground to her right rose. A rickety set of wooden steps ran up the bluff to Random House. It took nearly thirty minutes to wind her way to Whitmore's boundary.

The trust paid for a gardener to come to Witt's End once a week. It was a luxury the Witt's couldn't afford. Whitmore's grounds were overgrown, the formal flower beds smothered in a riot of weeds. The little chapel had nearly disappeared under a mass of ivy. The wisteria walk was impassable. Neither fountain was working, and only the grass near the house was mowed.

Jason was on his way out. He opened the door to the old servants' quarters seconds before she could knock. He saw no reason why people wouldn't be visiting at back doors at seven thirty on a Monday morning. After all, it was the kind of thing that people around here did all the time.

"Mom's in the sun room. Just tell her I let you in," he gestured vaguely. "I have some errands to run and then I'm off to work."

"You know, I'm beginning to think Esposito is right about our lack of concern about our security issues," Cerridwen observed dryly.

Jason shrugged, unconcerned. "Yeah. But you're you. And unless you koshed yourself on the head, I don't think I have anything to worry about." He left with a wave and a jingle of keys.

William Witt had dreams of Neo Gothic glory. So he had always referred to Joan's favorite room as the solar. Following generations simply called the two story glass construction the sun room. Joan had filled it with large plants and kept it warm and slightly humid year round. It was also the home of her standing embroidery frame which she used for larger projects.

Joan was sitting at it turned so that so the light through the glass fell over her shoulder. She looked up when Cerridwen knocked on the door frame. “Good morning. You’re up early.” She snipped a thread with her scissors and re-threaded her needle.

“I’ve been very restless lately. Byproduct of the concussion, they say.” Cerridwen, wandering the room, came to a stop in front of a large, long-leafed evergreen. “This is pretty. What is it?”

“It’s an oleander. It will bloom in another month or so. It does it fairly regularly. I think it’s the temp in here.”

“It’s huge.” It stood just a little taller than Cerridwen, not taking the planter into account.

“It’s years old. It used to stand in the estate office down the hall. Did you come all this way so early to discuss my house plants?” Joan asked with mild amusement.

“I had the oddest thought at about three this morning.” Cerridwen walked around behind Joan so she could see the work in progress on the frame. An incomplete image of the Green Man sprawled across the fabric. The fountain had been sketched into the foreground. The bedding plants around it were already rendered in loving detail.

“Did you?” Joan knotted her thread.

“I was thinking how old my house is. And then I started to wonder how many keys to my house are just lying around.”

“Keys?” Joan paused mid-stitch.

“Yeah.” Cerridwen settled in a threadbare armchair, tucking her feet under her. “I think at least one of the original keys is unaccounted for. And since the locks have never been changed, I suppose they would still work.”

Joan kept her eyes on her work, the needle flashing as it moved in and out. “There are only three keys to the main door, to the best of my knowledge. I remember the fuss when Constance had the copy made. I assume you can account for those.”

"But there are other doors. There were originally two keys to the conservatory's outside door. And, do you know, I can only lay my hands on one." She watched Joan's face, waiting for a reaction. The beginnings of a frown were interrupted by a bell. It was a more pleasant sound than Cerridwen's doorbell. It was produced by a real bell and a pull chain rather than an electrical monstrosity. She fumed as Joan went to answer it.

There had been the briefest flicker on Joan's face. It might have been panic. It wasn't what she had expected, but she could have worked with it. She needed to know what Joan knew about that key and, more importantly, who had it. She had to get rid of the interruption and wrench the conversation back around to the missing key.

Plans changed abruptly when Joan returned to the sun room with Jane and Detective Esposito. Jane's expression did not change, but something about her eyes told Cerridwen she was in for a lecture at the earliest opportunity. Esposito's eyes slid over her, noting her presence, but not reacting to it.

Joan dragged her chair out from behind the embroidery frame and waved them to sit. They chose to present a united front side by side on the settee. Esposito pulled a notebook out of a pocket and flipped it open. Jane carried a manila envelope.

"First, I need to ask you if you remember the date of Mary Paul's disappearance," Jane used her professional voice. It contained none of the humor of her everyday tone.

"Well, it's silly to call it a disappearance. But no, I can't remember the exact date that she left. It was summer and it all runs together. I would say she left somewhere near the beginning of August. But I wouldn't swear to it." Joan shrugged. Her tone was carefully neutral.

"A missing person report was filed on August 17. I would call that closer to the end of the month. Can you tell me why Constance Frey felt it was necessary?" Jane asked. Esposito observed.

"No, I can't. And I was unaware that she had. There was no need. She wasn't missing. She simply left." Joan fumed.

Jane remained impassive. Reaching inside she pulled out two small clear plastic packets.

"I am going to show you two items. I want you to tell me if you can identify them." She handed one little packet to Joan who took it and turned over a few times.

"It's a piece of fabric. A cotton silk blend, I would say." Joan squinted at it through the plastic. She was in her element. If there was one thing Joan knew, it was fabrics. "Varying shades of red and black. The piece is too small to be sure, but I would say it was a floral pattern. Printed, not woven. If I had to guess, I would say roses."

"Have you seen it before?" Jane asked.

Joan frowned in concentration as she turned the little package over in her hands. "I can't say that I have. But then one sees so many fabrics. If I had seen it some time ago I would have no cause to recall. The edges seem to be rotted rather than cut. It's either been buried or left somewhere very wet."

Cerridwen had a suspicion of where that fabric had been "buried." She watched the detectives closely, but neither of them was giving anything away. Jane accepted the packet with the slip of fabric in it and handed Joan a slightly smaller packet. Cerridwen leaned forward, trying to see what was in it. It was an earring. A brushed silver orb dangled from a matching stud, the two joined by a delicate filigree triangle.

"It's an earring," Joan stated. "A Monet earring from the 60s. Very popular when I was a kid. Very collectible now. Goodness, it's even signed. Mary had a pair just like this. She was wearing them the last time I saw her." She froze and the color drained from her face. "Where did you get this?" It came out a whisper.

"You are certain Mary Paul owned an earring like this and that she was wearing it the last time you saw her?" Jane's voice was even, professional, devoid of any emotion.

"Yes, yes." Joan's voice shook. "But where did you get it?"

"It was in the tree."

"But they were Mary's favorite. She would never have lent them. The only way that they could have ended up in that tree..." Jane broke off and shook her head. "No. It can't be her. It cannot be her. She went away." It was flat denial voiced with the stubbornness of a child.

"There are other ways that the earring could have gotten into the tree. And we are open to those possibilities. But we have to investigate the possibility that the woman in the tree is Mary Paul." Jane watched Joan closely. Joan handed back the earring.

"No." Again, the inflection was childish. "Mary left. She was ill and needed a rest. We had to go on without her." It was as if she repeated something often said to her. This was new information. No one had mentioned Mary Paul being ill before. Cerridwen slid a little lower in her chair hoping that the detectives would forget she was there.

"Did she tell anyone that she was leaving or where she was going?" Esposito's question was casual, conversational in tone.

"I don't know. She didn't tell me. But adults often don't think to tell children things."

"Was it like her to overlook you in that way?"

"Things get forgotten when you're in a hurry. Even people." Jane fidgeted.

"She was in a hurry?" Jane asked.

"I don't know." Joan twisted her skirt. "She was sick. She had to go away."

"Why was her friend unaware of this?"

"I don't know. Perhaps they were not as close as Ms. Frey liked to think." Joan tone was waspish.

"Did she pack her things? Or did she leave them here?" Esposito took up the questions again.

Joan flinched. Another short sharp twist of the skirt. Cerridwen began to wonder if the skirt or Joan would fray first. The normally calm woman was beginning to unravel.

"She left some things. Anyone might forget a few things when they have other things on their minds."

"Did she have something else on her mind?" he probed again.

"She had been upset. Something was bothering her." Joan's voice got smaller. "She was worried."

"About what? Do you know?" It was Jane's turn to ask a question.

"What do people ever get upset about? Money, a bad break up, the possibilities are endless."

Esposito came to point. "What made you think of those two possibilities?"

Cerridwen wondered if the choice to use the same word was deliberate. Jane did it to her sometimes when she was trying to win an argument.

Joan was having none of it. "I'm sure I don't know." For a split second there were two Joans. Then the frightened child was gone, the old Joan was back, confident, firm. The sudden change was unnerving. "If you will excuse me, there are some things that I need to get done this afternoon." She got up and the twist in her skirt fell loose, revealing a mass of wrinkles down one side.

Esposito had another question. "Where are the things she left behind?"

Joan flinched again but pressed on. "There is a box or two somewhere. I'll see if I can lay my hands on them when I have a spare moment."

And just like that, the three of them found themselves standing in the portico, the massive oak doors of Whitmore closed firmly behind them.

"We need whatever it is that Mary Paul left behind," Jane told the door.

"We could get a warrant, but it's going to take a while. And if we have to search for it, that will take time as well. That place is huge." Esposito took a step back looking at the three story French Gothic fantasy. "How would we even know what was hers?"

"I would wait till Jason came back and ask him," Cerridwen offered. They both turned to look at her. "It's the quicker option and the easiest, probably."

The two detectives looked at each other. There was a moment of silent communication and then Esposito turned and walked towards the unmarked car parked in the weedy gravel drive.

"What were you doing here?" Jane asked. It was not lost on Cerridwen that she used the same tone she had with Joan.

"I came to visit Joan, obviously."

"At a time when you would usually be neck deep in work. At a time when any interruption would be met with violence and repeated screams of the word deadline? I know you too well." Jane projected calm disbelief. "It was pretty clear you were not happy that we showed up. What were you up to?"

Cerridwen surrendered to the inevitable. "There is another key to Witt's End."

"And?"

"The last anyone knows of it, it was in Mary's possession. I thought it might have been how my assailant got into the house. And the only link I have to Mary is Joan."

"So you came over here to browbeat Joan rather than bring this information to me? Even though I am clearly in a better position to do something about it?" Jane's voice never lost its professional calm, but there was a certain tightness around her mouth.

"That doesn't necessarily follow," Cerridwen protested.

"Yes, Cerridwen, it does follow that a trained police detective is more qualified to deal with an investigation. If I had had that information going in, I might have been able to find out where that key was. It would certainly have changed how I approached the situation." Jane made an effort to soften her words. "It's not a book, honey. You cannot move these people around at will and expect them to do what you want. They will not fall willingly into what you consider the best possible plot line."

That stung.

"I don't think that way. I had a question and I looked for an answer. Maybe I looked in the wrong place, but that doesn't mean I see people as cardboard cutouts." Cerridwen fought not to snap at Jane and nearly lost. "You could be accused of the same thing," she pointed out. "That really wasn't the way to spring that earring on Joan."

"When people are unprepared for a question, they give more away. I am trying to solve a murder here."

"So it *was* murder." Cerridwen jumped on the information.

"Well, as you said, it's unlikely she put herself in that tree. Although if someone could tell me the cause of death, I would be a lot happier."

"Joan was really upset."

"There really isn't a way to do my job without upsetting people. Just keep the theories theoretical please. And trust me to do my job. Now go home and stay out of trouble for a few hours. Okay?" Jane started to walk towards the car. Cerridwen meant to let her go, but her character got the better of her.

"Jane." She waited for her friend to come back. "Mary wasn't just one of Witt's hangers-on. He was employing her as an accountant. Her disappearance occurred after she found discrepancies. If Joan overheard or saw something, that may be why money was her first thought."

"How did you find this out?"

"My Grandmother's diary," Cerridwen said.

"Your Grandmother's diary. Really?" Jane's disbelief was palatable. Cerridwen stared back with wide eyed innocence. That it was the truth made it a little easier to pull off. "Well, at least you didn't get that from talking to a possible murderer."

"Joan was eleven at the time. You can't possibly think she killed Mary."

"Stranger things have happened. Just please behave till I get home tonight." Jane didn't wait for an answer, but turned and got in the car.

Cerridwen watched the two detectives drive out Whitmore's gate, then walked home the way she had come, winding along the bottom of the garden and then up to the back of the house. She wondered how you would track a fifty year old embezzlement. She would ask Felix. Then she thought better of it. She would ask Teddy. It was the sort of thing he would know. It wasn't until she reached the terrace that she noticed an overdressed and impatient Fred sitting in one of her lawn chairs under the pergola.

Chapter 13

Cerridwen took in the black slacks, dress shirt, and polished shoes. "Aren't you a little overdressed to babysit?" she said by way of greeting.

"Aren't you a little old to be sulking?" Fred asked.

"There is a difference between sulking and contemplation. I am thirty years old, but one little head wound and suddenly I can't be left alone for an hour. People are passing me off to each other like a baton, for heaven's sake." She dropped in the chair beside him.

"You're looking at it the wrong way. You're Gerry's family, so you're our family, too, now. Which means we have the God given right to hang around you and squish stuff that shouldn't be around you. It's not that we don't trust you. It's that we don't trust the rest of the world."

"Stuff?" she asked.

"Stuff, people, whatever." He waved a hand dismissively.

"And who watches Teddy while you watch me?"

"Well, Teddy has good days and bad days,"

“All of Teddy’s days are good. His ‘spells’ are an excuse for him to do whatever he wants. And Gerry is here mostly to keep him out of jail.”

“Good to know.”

“Sorry, I’m in a mood. I got caught up in a puzzle and had to be reminded, gently, politely, but firmly, that people are not puzzle pieces. It was a bit of a blow to my ego. Also, turns out police investigations are equal parts ugly and tedious. Why are you dressed like that?”

“Like I’m dressed to tend bar at a pub called the Gargoyle? Which I am. Drive me to work? We’ll get there early, we can have lunch, or breakfast, and you can tell me all about your wounded ego and people shaped like puzzle pieces.”

A little while later they settled into a booth at the back of the Gargoyle, much to the great interest of Fred’s coworkers. The interior was an odd mix of Goth and metal. It was the first time Cerridwen had been there and she spent a moment studying the décor before looking at the menu, what there was of it.

“Well, if your ego needs a boost, you could probably get it from the bus boy,” Fred offered.

Cerridwen glanced up at him and then at the young man clearing a table a few yards away. He met her gaze and then blushed as he knocked over a glass.

“What does the bus boy have to do with my ego?”

“You don’t see it.”

“See what?”

Fred laughed and shook his head. “You smiled at him when we passed him on the way in and he walked into the wall.”

“I don’t think hand eye coordination is his strong suit.” She went back to her menu.

Fred was incredulous. “You own a mirror, right?”

Cerridwen sighed. “Let me tell you a secret. How men react to her is not always a woman’s first thought. Or even her second. The reason being most women don’t think of themselves as objects.”

“But you are aware you have effect?”

"Yes. But to be completely honest, a compliment from another woman means more. Most women dress to impress other women. They appreciate it more."

"I doubt that," Fred said.

"No, it's true. You might notice that I look nice today," she pointed out.

"Was that a hint?'

"But you will not say 'I love your boots' or 'that red is really good on you,' for example."

"Probably not," he agreed.

"And you will never say 'adorable shoes.'"

"I will not make the obvious point that you're wearing boots. So all this is for who?" Fred made a sweeping gesture.

"For me. You're just along for the ride."

"And what about Thomas?"

"He isn't here. I think I need something fried and fattening. How about you?"

"You know what I mean."

"You mean his ambition to marry me when he grows up?" Cerridwen thought for a moment. "I am both flattered and deeply disturbed."

Fred shook his head despairingly. "I warned him not to come off too stalkerish."

"No, that's not the problem."

Fred waited but she didn't elaborate. "Well, what is the problem?" he prodded.

"Among other things, I have been told that I am not the kind of girl that boys fall in love with," she said.

"You're kidding, right? What is that even supposed to mean, for Christ sake? What idiot told you that self-serving, pseudo-intellectual bullshit? No, wait, don't tell me. Two guesses. If I guess correctly, I get his home address and a length of lead pipe." Fred leaned across the table.

"Depends on what you plan to do with that pipe."

"Unimportant. I'll tell you who said it. It was either a guy you refused to sleep with or an ex with a tiny penis."

"I'm not answering that. But I'm not saying that your second guess is wrong."

"No, you're not the kind of girl boys fall in love with. Sweetie, you're the kind of woman a man gives his right arm to be with. And anyone who says otherwise is just that—a boy. So there, problem solved."

"I would always come after Thomas' music. And I've played second fiddle to a man's grand passion before. I discovered it's not something that I enjoy. I'm not particularly good at it, either," Cerridwen said.

Fred laughed. "I could see how it wouldn't suit you. And again, your ex was a boy, not a man. But I don't think you would come second. Music's not really a passion for Thomas. Music is kind of like breathing for him. It would be like saying you came second to oxygen. Sure, he needs to breath, but he won't feel about air like he feels about you." Fred sat back, the universe rearranged to his satisfaction.

Cerridwen shut her menu and laid it on the table. "Why do I feel like I'm getting a job interview and a pep talk at the same time?"

Fred leaned across the table. "Do you want to know a secret? Being in a band sucks. There really is no way to communicate how hard it sucks. And do you want to know why?"

"I have a strong suspicion you're going to tell me."

"First off," Fred counted on his fingers. "It's fine when you're a twenty something, fresh out of college. But when you're closing on thirty and you're still a guy with a day job and a band on the side, people start to think you never grew up. 'Cause if you have time to practice and drive around and play shows in dive bars, then you must have a lot of time on your hands. Time that grownups spend with family, and friends, and mortgages, stuff like that. So, if you got the time for this, must not be anything important going on in your life."

"People always make that assumption about artists, any kind of artist. People tell me how jealous they are of all my spare time, 'cause God knows what I do isn't really work," Cerridwen sympathized, but she really couldn't see where he was going with this.

"That is just one part of the suck." Fred held up another finger. "The real downer is what a money pit the whole thing is. Equipment, you're looking at six hundred to a thousand dollars per band member before you start. Now, maybe you get lucky and hook up with some guys that have their gear already. Transportation, you have to haul all that gear to the shows. That's gas, maintenance, and insurance, and something big enough to hold all of that gear. And if you go on the road, food and lodging, all of that comes out of pocket. What all this investment gets you is a string of gigs where, if you're very lucky, you break even."

"It does suck, but it's nothing different. Most art forms are a money-losing proposition until you hit the big leagues. Half the time people want it for free and get angry when you want to be paid." Cerridwen shrugged. She'd had this conversation more times than she could count. Hell, she'd been in that very situation more times than she could count. "Is that why Gerry says you're humoring them? Because you figure it's not going anywhere."

"See, that's the thing. I was humoring them." Fred pushed away from the table. "But we could actually hit the big leagues. Gerry is pretty damn good. Thomas has a lot of talent for writing music as well as performing it. The both have charisma. Well, Gerry does when he feels like it. Thomas can keep the rapt attention of a whole room of kindergartners. And he's got drive." Fred ran his fingers through his hair. If it had been a little shorter it would have stood on end. His sleeve rode up and he tugged it down over his tattoo. "He could drag us all the way to the top if he wants to."

"Is that a bad thing?" Cerridwen asked. She wasn't sure if she was amused or exasperated with Fred. Maybe she would wait till he made his point before she made up her mind.

"I haven't decided it yet. I like being a club musician and playing the odd studio gig now and then. I don't know if the big time is what I want. It's big and scary and new. And it is coming up way too fast. And that's where you come in." Fred grinned sheepishly. Now Cerridwen understood, and she had a hard time not laughing.

"You want me to marry him so he won't make a push for the big time."

"No, no. You don't have to marry him. Unless you want to. Just string him along for a while. Okay, that sounded bad. What I mean is, just see where it goes. And give the rest of us a little breathing room." Fred shrugged.

"I can't figure out if you're trying to further his cause or sabotage his career. I don't know that I'm comfortable with either." She knew she should be irritated, but the more she thought about it, the funnier it got.

"Not sabotage—just slow him down a little. That's all I'm asking." Fred wiggled his eyebrows at her.

"You don't want him to get a girlfriend. You're looking for a roadblock." Cerridwen made an effort to extract herself from the quagmire of a conversation. "Can we talk about something else? Maybe something a little less personal?"

"So why were you moving people around like puzzle pieces?"

"I said less personal."

"Then what?"

She frowned at him. The bus boy nearly upended the basket of bread he was setting on the table between them. Fred looked at the basket and then at Cerridwen as if this all proved his point somehow.

"It goes back to a game that Jane and I started playing shortly after she moved in. She tells me the bare bones of an investigation, and I take that and come up with what I think is the best plot to fit the facts. And I am right a surprising amount of the time."

"How do you pull that off?"

Cerridwen shrugged. "In Teddy's words, I have an agile mind. You have to have a certain understanding of human nature to be a writer. Sometimes it comes in useful in other ways. Really, I just throw out the most twisted explanation of the facts I can. It's like a thought exercise, very abstract. "

"But this time is different because the body is found right at your front door." Fred caught on quick. "Right after someone cold cocked you in your own house."

"Someone who was searching for something written the year Mary disappeared. And Jane is close to proving that the woman in the tree in Mary."

"How close?"

"The woman in the tree was wearing an earring that like one Mary owned. An earring that Joan remembers as her favorite."

"Did Joan tell you that?"

"No, I was there when Jane and her partner showed up. I wanted to know what Joan knew about a key to my house I can't account for."

"A key would certainly explain how your attacker got in the house."

"And Joan knows where that key is. I'm almost certain of it. There was a moment before we were interrupted. She said she had no idea. She wouldn't look at me when she said it."

"But you were whacked on the head before Thomas climbed that tree. I remember. I was there. I still haven't got my ball back."

"Stop whining and buy a new one." Fred just grinned at her. "The graffiti started about a month before that. Or I should say started again. There were one or two incidents shortly after Mary's disappearance."

"Whatever stirred this guy up started before the skeleton was found. Jane has no way of knowing what that is," Fred reasoned.

"Jane telling me to stop treating this like a plot is her way of saying don't stick your neck out. And I don't intend to. I will find out what Joan is so spooked over, though."

"We know why Joan is spooked. Or at least we have a damn good idea."

"She couldn't have done it. Not on her own. Anyway, she was only eleven at the time," Cerridwen objected. "It's possible that she saw something. She may even have been a part of whatever happened to

Mary, but I can't think she was responsible for all of it. Unless…" Her mind began to rework the information before she stopped herself. "No, I have to remember that possible plot lines are not facts. Joan is a real person. And it doesn't explain the missing money. As a child Joan wouldn't have had the access necessary to make off with the money."

"Joan has some serious trauma," Fred pointed out. "And that doesn't come from nowhere. Something caused it. Probably whoever was robbing Witt blind."

"If I figure out what, or who, caused it, I'll know what happened to Mary. And who has my key," Cerridwen said.

"You're going to do all of this from a safe distance, of course," Fred stressed.

"Of course."

After lunch, Cerridwen went home to get some work done herself. If Jane wanted her to keep her nose out of it all, then she would keep her nose squeaky clean. Besides, it wasn't as if Cerridwen had loads of free time to fill.

Recharged from a decadent lunch, she settled down to do battle with her arch nemesis once again. With less than ten thousand words to go, she could see the light at the end of the tunnel. Norland was coming to a messy end in a high speed chase when the doorbell shrieked. She turned the music up and pressed onward.

It continued for a while. Then changed to short brutal screams as someone stabbed the button over and over. She ignored it, slaughtering Norland with short, sharp words. The ear shattering noise stopped. It was replaced almost immediately with a loud pounding. Well, now she knew it wasn't Hawkner. Ann would die before endangering the glass in the front door that way.

Cerridwen came to the end of a sentence, pressed save and, with an irritated mutter, went to answer the front door. Jason Witt almost fell in when she opened the door.

"What the hell went on this morning? What did those cops say to my mother?"

"And hello to you, Jason. How are you this afternoon?" Her calm greeting brought him up short. Reminding him of his manners gave him a chance to take a breath and calm down.

"Hello, Cerridwen," he said with brittle courtesy. "My mother has completely flipped her lid. Would you know why, by any chance?"

"I would say I have some idea, yes. Would you like to come in and talk about it over a cup of tea?"Cerridwen continued in a mild tone. Jason growled and headed for the kitchen. She cut him off and led him into the grand salon. "Have a seat. I'll be right back."

She left him glowering on the sofa. Shutting the kitchen door firmly behind her, she set the kettle on the stove and reached for the phone. Jane answered on the third ring as Cerridwen put cups and the tea pot on a tray.

"Hello."

"Jason Witt is freaking out on our sofa. He wants to know what you did to upset his mother."

There was a beat of silence. "How upset is he?"

"He was more stampy-yelly than stabby-stabby, if that's what you're worried about. He has since retreated to painfully polite. But I have no idea how long he'll keep that up. And you might not want to ask about searching the house just yet."

"We don't have enough yet to ask for a warrant. We'll wait till he calms down."

Cerridwen peaked around the door frame, which only gave her a view of the hall and a sliver of the salon. "That could take a while."

"I'll be right there."

"Any suggestions what I should do with him in the mean time?"

"Stall." The phone went dead.

"Well, that's helpful." Cerridwen remarked to the unresponsive instrument. "And how does she suggest I stall without touching on subjects that upset him, and which I am supposed to be avoiding?" With the tea steeping in the pot, Cerridwen carried the tray into the room where Jason continued as if she had never left.

"All I want is to understand why my mother is suddenly around the bend."

"The last few days have been stressful for everyone. Even more so for Joan because she knew Mary Paul. It's awful to think of something like that happening to someone you cared about." Cerridwen tried to soothe him.

"It's more than that, I think." He paused for a moment, weighing his options. "There is something I'm not supposed to know about." His anger had dissipated, and now he was in the mood to confide in someone. Jane was still several minutes away. How did you stall someone who was determined to spill their guts? *And what is it about me*, Cerridwen wondered, *that makes them pick me?*

"At some point in her teens Mom had an 'incident.'" Jason made air quotes. "I'm not sure what happened, but it involved therapy."

"She was hurt?" Cerridwen couldn't help asking. Had Mary's killer made an attempt on Joan as well?

"Not physical therapy," he clarified. "There is a letter to Grandpa from some kind of doctor. He talks about her mental stability and her possible Electra complex. She is so wrapped up in that tree spirit story. It's a fairy tale. And all this time she believed it on some level. I think Mom saw something or knows something, and that story is how she dealt with it."

"I think you need to tell this to Jane. She would have a better idea of how to deal with it," Cerridwen said. And if he told Jane instead of her, then Jane couldn't be mad at her for sticking her nose in. Of course, she might not get to hear what he had to say about Joan either. Drat. It didn't look like she would have to choose.

Jason kept talking. "Having that idea messed with is seriously messing with her. Mom is usually a rock. Calm and competence personified. And now she's acting like she has PTSD. I just don't know what to make of it."

"Have you talked to her about it?"

"I've been afraid to. She's been off somehow ever since they found that thing in the tree," Jason muttered. "And that stupid graffiti popping up again hasn't helped. It's gotten worse since the cops were here this morning. She was mumbling to herself and wringing her hands. I've never seen anyone wring their hands before." Jason turned his tea cup round and round in his hand.

Was Joan really that disturbed by this morning's visit? Cerridwen worried. "You left her alone like that?"

"Oh, no. I left Stone with her," Jason said.

Fabulous, he left his traumatized mother alone with a person that wanted nothing more than to question her extensively about the event that caused it. She was about to point this out to him when she heard the front door open. She excused herself and met Jane in the hallway.

"What took you so long? Jason Witt is in there ready to spill his guts. Already spilling them, in fact. Who's this?" Cerridwen noticed the man who had followed Jane into the house.

He spun slowly, tool bag hanging from his hand. He let out a long, low whistle as he took in the entryway. "Some place you got here," he said.

"Thank you," Cerridwen answered, the manners drilled into her since birth coming to the surface automatically. She emphasized her earlier question by pointing at him and raising her eyebrows, a trick she had picked up from Thomas.

"Carl. He's here to do something about the lock to the conservatory to door. What is Jason spilling his guts over?"

"His mother's disturbed mental state, including earlier episodes, and their possible connections to dead chicks who hang out in trees," Cerridwen rattled off. "If you go about it right, he might even let you search the house. I'd hurry, though. He left her alone with Stone, and there's no telling what he's asking her."

Jane did not swear, but it was obvious she wanted to. She went into the room where Jason sat and closed the door with a finale, solid sounding click.

Cerridwen turned to Carl. "So, what are you doing to my conservatory door?"

Chapter 14

Cerridwen took it easy Tuesday morning. The lock to the side door had been replaced, a process that had Carl alternately humming and swearing. But apparently a lock that old could not be re-keyed, so the whole thing had had to come out and the Historical Society be damned. He had managed to drum up a reproduction lock somewhere and thought it a good match. Possibly the Hawkner wouldn't notice.

As far as Cerridwen was concerned, the world could take care of itself today. She turned off the phone, turned up the music, and fired up her laptop. She spent the morning tying up loose ends and rearranging her timeline. She got enough work done that she was only slightly annoyed when there was a rap on the back door.

Felix stood on the terrace with an armful of flowers and bags from a local deli. He submitted graciously to her hugs. He politely did not mention that she had creased his shirt in the process.

"I knew you were working when your phone went to voice mail. But it's nearly two o'clock and I'm dying to know what's been going on while I was gone. Of course, I know I'm committing a cardinal sin by cutting into work time, do I brought lunch to grease the wheels," he said.

Cerridwen stepped back to let him into the kitchen.

"And I brought flowers. I thought the ones I sent would be about to expire. Now, tell me all about the head wound and the dead body," he said.

Lunch was excellent. Felix didn't like to cook, but he liked good food and was willing to pay for it. She filled him in on the past week while they ate. He informed her he thought the whole incident interesting but badly plotted.

"I don't care for the several decades of lag," was his opinion. "Too long with nothing happening. And I don't hold with coincidence. It's too contrived."

"What coincidence?" Cerridwen wasn't sure what he was talking about.

"That's the really funny part. It's the damnedest thing, but I know who Thorn Apple is." Felix's smile was irritatingly smug

"How? You weren't even here."

"That's the coincidence. Thomas called to see if I could keep an eye on you and Teddy while he did the shopping. Really, I think you should marry that boy. I mean seriously, if he's willing to do your grocery shopping," Felix said.

That was twice in as many days someone had suggested she marry Thomas. It was a conspiracy. "Really? That's your criteria for marriage? Whether or not they're willing to do the shopping?" she said.

"Scoff if you want, but it's a necessary part of life. And think of all the work you could get done if you're not always running to the store all the time. I mean, I don't do that myself, but I hear other people do it all the time. Thomas mentioned that people are leaving dead bodies lying around. I was at this lunch thing and the man next to me overheard the conversation. And who did he turn out to be but Teddy's hippie photographer. Only he's not a hippie really. Quite respected, actually. David Thorn, he's putting out a coffee table book. A retrospective sort of thing, I believe."

"Did you get contact information? You have to tell Jane."

"Well, here's the thing. I brought him home with me." Felix was pleased with himself, really a fairly common state of affairs.

Cerridwen was stunned. "You brought a stranger, one possibly connected with a murder, home with you? Felix, isn't that a bit out there, even by your standards?"

"I didn't know he was connected with the murder. Technically I didn't know there had been a murder. Thomas made a throwaway comment about leaving bodies lying around and then hung up on me. Really, dear, you'll have to do something about his communication skills."

"And people leave bodies that have not been murdered just lying around in the normal course of things," Cerridwen pointed out.

"Well, consider the group of people we're talking about," was Felix's comeback. "David and I got to talking about the neighborhood. He mentioned that he was part of Witt's little commune. He's still trying to track down some people to sign releases for the photos he wants to use. And I said why didn't he come and stay. I have plenty of room and no idea that the body was Mary Paul. It's probably going to come as a shock to him. Perhaps I can get Jane to tell him."

"She might actually prefer that. I got a lecture on sticking my nose in yesterday. My advice is to hand everything to her and keep yourself out of it as much as possible," Cerridwen said.

"Excellent advice. Want to come to dinner tonight and meet him? You can bring the boys with you."

"Dinner for, what, six on short notice? You don't even cook."

"Oh, more. The Sands Girls will have to come." It was a source of amusement to the Sands that Felix insisted on calling them girls at their age. "And Stone is always good entertainment value. I'll get someone to cater. I'll throw money at them until food appears. And I can cook. I choose not to. Nothing formal, it's come as you are. A little wine, a little food, and we'll see what we shake out."

"But we're not going digging. We don't want Jane mad at us," she said.

"Of course not. The woman carries a gun, for heaven's sake. But it will naturally be on everyone's mind. And who are we to fight the natural flow of conversation?"

Give Felix his due, he did manage to find someone to provide dinner. There were appetizers and cocktails while a frazzled caterer unpacked dinner in the kitchen.

Thomas propped himself against the wall and watched Cerridwen watch everyone else. Her reactions to her friends' antics flickered openly across her face like she was watching a movie.

Fred came to stand beside him. "Careful. Look too much like a stalker and Gerry will take you out."

"I'd snap him like a twig," Thomas replied.

"I don't know. He's small but devious. And very attached to her. I think he could take you. In your sleep probably, with a step ladder, but I think he could do it. But that's not the only reason you should be careful."

"Oh?"

"Someone has done some damage. I don't think it's deep, but it won't make for an easy road."

Felix, making the rounds with his guests, chose this moment to insert himself into the conversation. "Whose death are we plotting? Or is that not your default topic of conversation? Making you the minority in this crowd."

"Fred thinks some guy did some damage to Cerridwen," Thomas said.

"Damage? I suspect you mean Ryan Little Dick. Excuse me, I meant to say Littleton. I don't know how that came out wrong. He tried. I wouldn't think it was more than skin deep, though. Do you want his home address?" Felix was ever the perfect host providing for his guest's every need.

"Do you have any lead pipe?" Fred wanted to know.

"I might have some lying about somewhere. It is a fairly old house, bound to be a bit of questionable plumbing." Felix saw nothing strange in this request.

"What did he do?" Thomas shifted away from the wall.

"I don't know exactly. Cerridwen simply started to avoid him and generally pretend he didn't exist. I could guess, of course. But I couldn't say for sure. Oh dear, Ruby and Stone have cornered poor David." Felix sailed off to intercept the chiffon battleship. Thomas and Fred trailed after him in case he needed an extra tug to haul her to dock.

It proved unnecessary. Thorn simply smiled and walked away. Ruby was undeterred, turning the full force of her anecdote on Stone. She pinned the biographer to the fireplace surround with words as Thorn made his escape.

From what little she had heard of him, Cerridwen was expecting David Thorn to be larger than life. In reality, he was more economy size. Cerridwen wondered idly if he had what it took to haul a body into a tree. Sparing with words and nearly stingy with gestures, the photographer was an extension of the camera he carried. He watched and recorde, but rarely interacted. He laughed and snapped a picture when Ruby struck a dramatic pose against the mantelpiece. It was the first sound he had made since introductions.

Cerridwen settled with her drink in the shadow of an overachieving potted palm. Felix decorated with the zealous abundance of a golden age Hollywood set. It left you waiting for a Busby Berkeley number to break out at any moment.

A click and a flash, and there was Thorn on the other end of the sofa. "You looked like your grandmother there for a moment," he said softly.

"How so?" Cerridwen set down her drink.

"The glare of death you gave me before you caught hold of yourself. 'Never photograph a woman without her knowledge,' she would say. "'I've worked too hard on my image to have it destroyed by some artsy brat with a camera.'" That woman forgot more about lighting than I ever knew." He examined his lens for imaginary smears. It was the longest speech he had made since they had met. She thought he was finished. Surely that burst of words must have exhausted him.

"She was a daughter of a great beauty and the product of the studio machine. She knew every angle, every trick. The shots of her were some of my best. And I'm not ashamed to admit it's because she told me what to do. With your permission, I would like to use them in my book." There, now he was done.

"You will have to approach the trustees of her estate. Everything is in trust and I make very few of the decisions," Cerridwen said.

"I brought something to trade." He slid something small out of his breast pocket and set on the couch cushion between them. It was creased and faded, as if it had spent a lot of time in that pocket. "That is the only photograph of Mary Paul I know of. She didn't like to have her picture taken. I thought that detective friend of yours might find it useful." He sat looking at the image for a moment. "Do they know it's her?" There was a wistful tone to his question.

"I don't know. I don't know that Jane would tell me if she knew for sure."

Thorn nodded and took a deep breath. He took off again, snapping pictures as he went, once again the impartial observer.

Jane couldn't accuse her of moving him about like a puzzle piece. While she was looking for the edge pieces, Thorn had simply jumped out of the box and walked away.

Chapter 15

An uncharacteristic storm had swept in last night with an unexpected foot of snow. It had shut down the entire city of Victoria. It had an ill effect on Cerridwen's already foul mood. She had finished her rough draft with plenty of time left for revisions. Only she didn't want to revise it. She wanted to fling her laptop out the window.

"I believe, upon reflection," she said to the chilly scene outside her window, "that it is complete and utter crap." She banged her head against the glass a few times in a halfhearted fashion. "I need distance. And alcohol." After a moment she added, "And chocolate." She had none of these things. The snow made acquiring them unlikely.

Her head thumped the glass again. It answered with a dull rattle of protest. Even the phone was discontented today, its usual jaunty ring sounding shrill and listless. She ignored it until Felix's wheedling voice came from the answering machine's speaker.

"I have wine."

It was enough. Cerridwen answered the phone. "You know me too well. What do I have to do for this wine?"

"Oh, I' m sorry, did you want some? I'm kidding, don't growl at me, woman. Come over here, have lunch, and don't think about work, dead women in trees, or overreaching Historical Societies all afternoon. Do that and you can have you very own bottle. We can discuss costumes for Joan's party."

"Shit, I'd forgotten." Yet another thing to worry about. Maybe she could dig something out of the closet. With three generations of wardrobe to choose from, Cerridwen was sure she could find something.

"Don't worry about it right now," Felix said. "Just come over here and get squiffy."

He didn't need to tell her more than twice. Cerridwen bundled up and struck out against the thick, wet mess of the court.

The large extended family that provided gardening services for the homes on the court was out in force. Men of varying ages were plying shovels all up and down the paths. Maria Irena was helping her grandfather check the mulch on the plantings.

"Maria, could you ask your grandfather a question for me?" The older Mr. Demetriov still refused to speak English, although Cerridwen was convinced he understood it. But the Demetriov family had been groundskeepers back when the Witt's could afford it. He or someone related to him might remember what she needed to know. "Does he remember a rope in the big oak at any point?"

There was a delay as Maria spoke to her grandfather in the peculiar mix of Spanish and Russian used by all the Demetriovs.

"He says what time are you asking after."

"1965, in the late summer to fall."

Another delay, and Mr. Demetriov shook his head.

"No, he says. No rope. But then they would hardly need it with that block and tackle hanging right there."

Cerridwen's surprise must have shown on her face. Mr. Demetriov grinned at her. "What block and tackle?" she asked.

This triggered a torrent of words. Maria translated in rapid bursts when her grandfather paused for breath. "It was from the turn of the century. The last one. They used the block and tackle when they put up the fountain. No room for a crane. They left it there. Had a swing hanging from it for a bit in the 50s."

"When did they take it down? Who took it down?" Cerridwen blurted.

"No one took it down, he says. It fell in a wind storm September or October of '65. That's why the east facing nymph has a chunk out of her head. It fell on her, didn't it? Caused quite the flap at the time. He says there was all kinds of arguing."

"Who was arguing about what? Gravity and wind don't seem to be arguable subjects." Although Cerridwen was sure that some would try. She waited through another lengthy exchange between Maria and her grandfather. Papa Demetriov shrugged by way of punctuation.

"He says the Lotus Eaters were of two minds about it all. That's what he calls Witt's hippies. Some thought it should be reinstalled or replaced because it was historic or some nonsense. The others thought the tree had shunned the symbol of human oppression."

"I did not know that trees shunned things."

"They don't. The just grow around or through things that get in their way. But some people, they think nature is like Disney." Maria shrugged in the same manner of her grandfather and turned back to her mulch. He had moved down the block to mumble lovingly over the rhododendrons. It appeared her audience was at an end. She set off again towards Felix's house.

A rope and pulley would certainly be easier than just a rope thrown over a branch. Had the pulley's destruction been a stroke of luck or a horrible surprise? It removed some of the evidence, of course, but it made it impossible to retrieve the grisly secret in the tree. Had the murderer meant to leave it there all along, or had there been no choice?

She had made it halfway across the court when a slushy snowball knocked her hat askew with a splat. Melting snow slid down her head and trickled down her neck. She turned slowly towards the source.

Gerry backed hurriedly away from her murderous look. "Sorry Cerridwen! Didn't mean to…"

Her own missile caught him square in the mouth. He fell backwards with a gargle. Fred chose the better part of valor and fled, leaving Gerry to fend for himself. She fired another slush ball as Gerry scrambled for shelter behind the lilacs. The frustration of the past weeks found an outlet as she gathered up more handfuls of the rapidly melting snow. Her gloves were wet through and her hat slid over one eye.

Thomas ran up the path behind her. Cerridwen heard him coming, turned, and flung the snow without taking the time to pack it. He blocked most of it with his arm.

"Please. Is that supposed to scare me? I work with small children. You're going to have to do be…"

She ran at him with a yell, crashing into him at speed. Predictably he didn't budge.

"What ya going for here?" He swayed only slightly as she dug in and shoved, her feet sliding on the compacted snow. "It's usually easier to just tell me what you want than to try and move me with brute force. Which you don't have. And studies show that it dramatically increases your chances of getting what you want."

"I want to knock you over!" She stated the obvious.

"Oh, is that all?"

Cerridwen realized what he was going to do a second too late. Thomas wrapped both arms around her and fell backwards into the snow bank. They landed with a sound that was half crunch, half splash. "Is that what you were after? I don't understand the reasoning. I'm not complaining, mind you."

She fought her way to an upright position and tried to push her hat out of her eyes. She pummeled him with cold, wet fists. He just laughed at her until she shoved a handful of slush down the front of his jacket.

"Guys, tone it down," Fred called over Thomas's howl of outrage. "You want the Hawkner to come out here and yell at us for lowering the tone of the neighborhood?"

"Yeah," put in Gerry. "She's going to be pissed enough when she sees someone built a snowman at her front gate. So low class."

"She has to know already. It's wearing that god-awful orange scarf she was wearing yesterday," Fred pointed out. "It's a bit of an odd shape. You know that's going to make her mad. Not only a snowman, but a poorly made one at that." He and Gerry laughed.

Cerridwen turned to look at the snowman leaning drunkenly against the pillar marking the edge of Gate House's property. It had an odd stooped appearance. The scarf was a painfully bright shade of orange.

"Maybe someone is trying to do the scarf in," Cerridwen suggested.

Thomas sat up and scooped handfuls of snow out of his jacket, nearly dislodging her in the process. "Who would want to kill a scarf? Also, who would want that scarf to begin with?"

"It's an attempt to be on-trend. But she doesn't understand trends. It is a longer and louder version of a designer one Mrs. Gray often wears. Probably cheaper as well."

"Isn't imitation the sincerest form of flattery?" Gerry combed clumps of snow out of his hair.

"That scarf could never be any form of flattery," Felix informed them as he sauntered down the path towards them. Thorn followed him closely, his ever present camera flashing and clicking. "We came to search for you. It doesn't usually take you a half hour to cross the court. Especially with a bottle of wine waiting on the other side. Are you in need of rescuing?"

"You and what army?" Gerry drove his taunt home with a snowball. Felix did not even flinch. He brushed snow off his dark topcoat. Unhurriedly he scooped up a handful of slush. Gerry tried to evade, but Felix had long arms. He caught Gerry by the collar and smeared the handful of snow liberally over his face.

Fred charged to Gerry's aid. After a brief struggle, the three of them landed in the snow with Felix on the bottom. "Ow! My dignity," cried Felix. By the time they had separated themselves, it was all-out war. The battle raged up and down the court, with the Demetriovs yelling encouragement to one side or the other by turns.

Cerridwen took Thomas hostage. He escaped by getting up and walking away. She and Felix charged after him to be turned back by rapid fire from Fred and Gerry. Thorn refused to join in, saying a photographer's role in a war zone was to record the carnage, snapping pictures all the while.

She cut Gerry off from his friends and cornered him against the stone wall running between the street and Hawkner's property. He faked right and then dashed to the left. He wasn't watching where he was going and ran into the snowman. He flung out an arm to catch himself and caught the scarf instead. It came untied and followed him to the ground, bringing the snowman's head with it.

The lumpy snow sculpture had started to melt and something dark broke the surface. Closer up it looked like fabric. The running battle had followed them across the road. Thomas swore, pushed between Cerridwen and the mutant snow person, while she and Gerry tried to untangle themselves. When he touched it, a chunk of crusted snow fell away. An arm in a dark tweed sleeve fell free limply.

Thomas tore at the crust of half melted snow. Gerry attacked the other side. Fred grabbed Cerridwen and pulled her face into his coat, but not before she saw a blue-tinged Ann Hawkner hauled free of her icy tomb. Over the roaring in her ears she could dimly hear Thomas swearing in English and Russian.

"It's not real," she told the front of Fred's coat. "People don't do things like that in real life.

Chapter 16

The flurry of activity that followed made the fuss over Mary Paul's discovery appear insignificant. It was obvious that the chance to revive Ms. Hawkner had long since been lost. The ambulance bundled her off in short order. Cerridwen had a fairly good idea where to, but she didn't want to think about it.

They were all questioned briefly and then herded into Felix's house. There they were separated and questioned in greater detail. Thorn turned over the memory card to his camera with a sigh, communicating his belief that he would never see it again. By dinner time they had been through three rounds of questioning, first with two uniformed officers, then by another officer that seemed to be of a higher rank. Finally Jane and Jesús arrived and it started all over again.

Felix had decided to treat the whole incident as yet another opportunity to entertain. Take out was delivered at about six p.m. There was quite the fuss involved in getting the delivery driver around the crime scene. Felix took the officers' refusal of food as a personal insult and was incensed that they flatly refused to let him serve anyone alcohol. When the mass of police cleared, he took it as a challenge to provide everyone still left with as much as alcohol as they could hold.

Thomas retreated to a darkened hallway with the drink that Felix had pressed on him. He wasn't even sure what it was. He braced his feet and slid down the wall to the floor. He downed his glass. Whatever it had been, it tasted terrible. He eyed the empty glass distrustfully and then flung it against the opposite wall. It made a satisfying crash and tinkle as it shattered.

"Do you feel better now?" Jane's voice came out of the darkness above him. He took a moment to think about the question as the music in his head changed to the full and sexy brass of classical jazz that always followed her. Not that modern crap—real jazz from the 20s.

"No," he said finally. "It doesn't."

"Well, we'll see how you feel when Felix realizes you just broke one of his eighty-dollar Swedish crystal glasses."

"I do not intend to tell him," he informed her with dignity. "How long was Hawkner in that snowman?"

"I don't know yet. Judging by the color she was, I would say a while."

"Like, hours? Or since last night?" Thomas eyed the shards of his glass. He should have kept it. Now he couldn't put anymore booze in it. Not that he was going to get drunk. It took a depressing amount of anything to put him under.

"Several hours at least. I can't give you an exact number. Time of death isn't exact. It's not like on TV where they can tell you to the minute. The best we'll ever get is a ballpark," Jane said. She dropped on to the floor besides him.

"What I need to know—" God, his hands were shaking. He took a deep breath and started over. "What I need to know going is, would she still be alive if I had noticed her sooner?" Jane stirred, but he kept on. "If we hadn't been screwing around, if we had paid more attention, would Ann Hawkner be alive right now?"

"I cannot tell you for certain, but my instinct says she was dead long before any of you showed up. I don't think there was anything you could have done differently." She dropped onto the floor beside him. They sat there in silence, the darkness pressed down on them.

"Jane, why do you trust me with Cerridwen?" He hadn't meant to ask that, but it had weighed on him.

"I wasn't joking when I said I knew what size underwear you wear. To be truthful, it's a gross understatement. I have everything about you that was ever entered into a computer from the day you were born. You haven't sneezed that I didn't know about it."

"Yeah, but what does that tell you about a person's character?" Thomas shrugged. "You don't know me from Schrödinger's cat."

"Maybe not, but Gerry and Teddy know you pretty well. In his lucid moments, Teddy is an excellent judge of character. And you're forgetting that I am a police officer. You would be amazed what people will tell an officer, even over the phone."

"Oh, dear God." Thomas covered his face with his hands as certain incidents in his past flashed before his eyes. "What have you heard?"

"Relax. Everyone spoke very highly of you, from your kindergarten teacher on up through Berkeley School of Music. And the double major is impressive. Your boss adores you. If I hadn't talked to your ex-girlfriend, I would have thought you were too good to be true. Although she had nothing bad to say about you, your replacement feels a little competitive still."

"There is no competition. We were awful together, and he makes her happy. And, for the record, I never said that song was about her. If she, or he, choose to jump to that conclusion, that says more about them than me. Just saying."

"Agreed." She turned to look at him. "And it is kind of obvious how disgustingly in love you are."

It was startling to hear it out load. He couldn't say he hadn't admitted it to himself, but he had tried very hard not to think about it.

"Disgusting , huh?"

"Downright sickening. Of course, it goes without saying," she continued in much the same tone. "If you screw up, I will kill you. And

I'd probably get away with it, too. But hey, no pressure." She patted him on the shoulder.

"Thanks a lot. That makes me feel much better. That was sarcasm, by the way."

"I'm sure it was. It's just that you're not very good at it," Jane said.

"You think so?" Thomas pulled his sleeves down over his wrists. Had his shirt gotten wet enough in the snow to shrink? Not that it was all that important.

"Well, if you were good at it, you wouldn't need to tell people it was sarcasm, now would you?"

"Your partner thinks it's too fast." He watched her out of the corner of his eye.

"Between you, me, and the wall, there is just a touch of jealousy on his part. It's Cerridwen's opinion that matters in the end. There is a difference between fast and wrong. And so far she hasn't been wrong but the one time that I know of. And I can't complain, she made up her mind about me just as fast. And low rent is nothing to sneer at, especially in this neighborhood."

"Christ doesn't like me." Between the dead body and the lack of alcohol Thomas was feeling a little morose.

"That might have something to do with your inability to get his name right."

"It's not an inability. I do it on purpose."

"I'll be sure to tell him that," Jane said. "I'm certain it will make all the difference. I wouldn't worry about the sour grapes. He'll get over it. He and Cerridwen and wouldn't suit at all. He doesn't get her sense of humor. Besides, he can't get involved with someone in the middle of a murder investigation. It looks bad when you go to trial. Makes the court think you're biased or something."

She used the wall to pull herself up and patted him on the head as she passed. "Besides, you're taller."

Chapter 17

Cerridwen studied the picture of Mary Paul as it lay on the kitchen table in the poor light of a sleety morning. She had given Jane the original before she left for work that morning. What Jane didn't know, didn't need to know, was that Cerridwen had scanned a copy before she handed it over.

It showed a dark-haired young woman of medium height on the steps of Whitmore House. She shared Cerridwen's grandma's poise and sense of style. Not surprising, as the two women had been friends. Mary knew how to pose and had a killer sense of style. Cerridwen winced at her own choice of words, but other than that, the photo didn't have much to tell.

Jane thought the image was clear enough it could be used for canvassing the area. But it was unlikely anyone would remember a particular day in August five decades later. There were various forensic techniques for photographs. But Jane doubted the image was detailed enough, even if the department's budget would stretch that far.

The message light blinked with a persistence that bordered on sulking. Cerridwen watched the sleet outside turn to wet, sticky snow. Ann Hawkner's strident tones filled the room.

"Miss Evans-Jones, I need to speak with you most urgently. It has come to the attention of the Historical Society that you had at least one of your locks changed. This action was not approved by the Society and while I understand it might be necessary, I must inquire as to whether or not the replacement is adequate. We have an obligation to uphold certain standards."

There was a moment of silence as if Ms. Hawkner was waiting for the answering machine to agree with her. "Please contact me as soon as possible," she insisted before she hung up.

Yeah sure, thought Cerridwen. *I'll get right on that. As soon as I find an Ouija board.*

She turned to set the kettle on the stove and swore at length as the doorbell made itself heard. She stamped towards the front of the house as the hellish tones reverberated through the hall. First thing tomorrow she was murdering that infernal device, and screw the Historical Society. Then she would have all the locks changed just to remind people that they were her locks.

She yanked the door open and came nose to nose with Joan. A wrinkled, worn, and slightly crazed Joan. Shaky hands seized the front of Cerridwen's sweater. She was less than proud that her first thought was for the cashmere being pulled out of shape.

"I found it. I didn't think it would be there, but it was." Joan's voice cracked on the edge of tears.

"What did you find?" Cerridwen pried fingers out of fabric and felt for her phone in her pocket for her phone. She had started to carry it everywhere in light of recent events. "Should I call Jane?"

"I don't know?" Joan's uncertain tone made it a question. Cerridwen tried to think. If it was information about Mary's disappearance, Jane would need to know. But would Joan be willing to confide in Jane?

"Whatever it is, Jane would know what to do," Cerridwen said, trying to reassure Joan and ease her into the house.

"I don't know what to tell Jane. What will she think?" Joan became more agitated. "I can't. I can't." This was getting them nowhere. The smart thing would be to call Jane, but Joan wasn't having any of it—or common sense or lucid thought, for that matter.

Cerridwen took a deep breath. It was best to remain calm while you did something stupid. "Can you show me what's wrong?"

"Yes, that would work. Come and see. Come see what he did. And then tell me what to do." Joan grabbed her hand and gleefully hauled Cerridwen out the door and down the steps. Cerridwen managed to pull the door shut behind her.

"Who, Joan? Who did what?" she begged.

Joan didn't answer, just pulled harder. They hurried around the south end of the court and up the drive to Whitmore. The closer they got to whatever it was, the more unwound Joan became.

Cerridwen struggled to catch her breath as Joan's grip propelled her up the stairs. *Clearly,* she thought, *this had not been her best plan of action.*

They came to one of the smaller bedrooms near the back of the house on the second floor. At first it looked like a closet. Cerridwen feared for a moment that Joan was going to shove her into it. Instead, Joan threw open the door, then backed fearfully away from it.

"There. All of it. It's still here. All of Mary's stuff is still here." Joan collapsed against the wall and sobbed into her tie-dyed skirt.

Cerridwen confronted a neat and tidy bedroom. If it wasn't for the layer of dust, she would have thought the inhabitant had just left. One silver earring, the mate to the one in Jane's possession, lay on the dressing table, catching the light slanting through the window behind it. A small pile of sagging cardboard boxes rested in the corner. It looked as if someone had simply moved out and forgot half their stuff.

"This where I saw her last." Joan's sudden calm was almost eerie. "I had no idea it would be the last time."

Cerridwen had no idea what to say. It was just as well Joan didn't want an answer.

"Mary was wearing that red dress with the roses printed on it. She had a cup of tea. She was doing her makeup at the dressing table. She used to let me play with the brushes. And then Thornapple came in." Joan went silent. She pressed her back against the wall and slid to the floor, staring through the doorway at something Cerridwen couldn't see.

"He didn't have his camera, which was strange. He always had his camera. He was carrying books instead. I'd never seen him with a book before and he had two." She was thinking out loud and Cerridwen was reluctant to interrupt the stream of consciousness. She couldn't let it pass though. Not when everyone was after books of one form or another.

"Do you know what books they were?"

"I don't know. It wasn't important at the time. He wanted to talk to Mary about something and Mary told me to leave. She said it nicer than that, but she made me leave. Told me we would do something later, but then she was sick. And then she was gone. I never saw her again. Thorn was there and he was angry about something. He left the next day. No one would tell me what happened. They might not have known. So wrapped up in themselves."

"Joan, who said she was sick? Did you see her when she was ill?" Joan wasn't listening. Cerridwen tried again. "Joan, what kind of illness was it?" Tears were running down Joan's face. Cerridwen was glad she had taken the time to find her phone this morning as she dialed Jane. They waited for Victoria's finest in the hall, the open bedroom door looming in front of them. The tears continued. Joan's distress was reaching a fever pitch.

"I was trying to figure out what was happening. That's why I did it. I'm so sorry. I didn't mean to. It was a mistake." Joan's voice had taken on a childlike quality. She gripped Cerridwen's hand in a crushing grip.

"You didn't mean to go in Mary's room?" She tried to gently retrieve her hand. As she slid away from Joan, her foot struck something unnoticed in the shadows, something heavy that rolled away in a slow curve.

Joan ignored the question and instead let go of Cerridwen and reached up to stroke her hair. The object came free of the length of fabric wrapped around it and dim light sparked off of Cerridwen's missing candlestick. Joan's shaky fingers probed the spot of on the back of the woman's head where the candlestick had made impact.

"I never meant to hurt you." The childish voice took on a pleading tone. "I thought you were someone else."

A cold wave of nausea over took Cerridwen. She wanted to believe she had misunderstood, but Joan kept talking.

"I only wanted to look at the journal. But someone else was there." The more familiar competent Joan was back. "Do you understand? Someone was already in your house when I got there. Someone else was looking for that journal."

People were coming up the front steps—official sounding people.

Cerridwen pushed past Esposito as he came down the hall. She was thoroughly sick in Joan's historic first floor powder room.

Joan that she had known all her life. Joan had broken into her house and assaulted her. And then showed up the next day with breakfast. Like nothing had happened.

Jane found her a short time later lying on the cool tile floor with a threadbare washrag on her forehead. The red top coat Cerridwen had convinced Jane to buy was a surreal note in the black and white bathroom. Neither of them spoke as Jane took the rag, wet it again, and dropped it back on Cerridwen's forehead. When she didn't respond, Jane took a pen out of an inner pocket and stuffed it in her hand.

"Do you want to tell me what happened?" She perched on the edge of the tub and waited.

Cerridwen pulled the rag down over her eyes. "I want to make it clear that I started this morning off minding my own business."

Jane clicked the pen several times. Why were nervous tics so soothing?

"Of course," she agreed. Cerridwen recognized Jane's soothing, professional voice, so different from the wry humor of the Jane she knew at home.

"Then Joan turns up and drags me over here. Shows me a room still full of Mary Paul's stuff. Just left there as if she'd just stepped out yesterday. Then Joan bursts into tears, confesses to koshing me on the head and says oh, by the way, there was someone else in my house that night. And then I threw up."

"Does she know who this person was?"

"She didn't say. You'd be better off asking her. Although be careful how you time it. She seems to be bouncing back and forth between present day and eleven year old Joan."

"It can happen with a traumatic event."

"Yes, but which traumatic event? There seems to be a surplus lately."

"My guess? Start with whatever happened to Mary and work down from there."

"It's horrifying." Cerridwen couldn't shake the nausea.

"That Joan's your attacker?"

"Well, yes, obviously. I had a full-blown anxiety attack over that, to be honest. But I was thinking how awful it must have been for Joan. Whatever did happen, it is clear that it happened when she was a child. The adults in her life failed her, Jane. In a big way. And there is no sign any of them noticed, let alone cared. Hell, a woman was murdered practically under their noses and they all just shrugged it off. Joan was a kid. Someone should have been taking care of her. They should have gotten her some kind of help."

"Someone tried, according to Jason. They sent her to that therapist."

"Yes, but they don't seem to have tried very hard. And it was after the fact. Whatever happened to her shouldn't have. She was a child and someone should have protected her. That is what parents' are for."

Jane seemed to have no answer to this. The lingering nausea reminded Cerridwen of something Joan had said.

"Someone told her Mary was sick."

"Who?"

"I didn't get it out of her. Joan said first Mary was sick and then she was gone. But if she hadn't seen Mary since that morning, someone had to have told her. Joan was looking for a journal. I don't know if she meant my grandmother's journal, but I don't know what else she would hope to find in my house. Give me a moment and I'll try again."

"No. I'll get it out of her. You're going home. I called Felix."

"Why?" Cerridwen lifted the rag to peer at Jane.

"Because I don't think you should be by yourself right now, and I have to work."

Cerridwen sighed and dropped the rag again.

"It won't be so bad," Jane told her. "It's Felix. He'll spend the afternoon pumping you full of food and wine."

"Right now the very thought makes me feel sick all over again. The past two weeks have been nothing but people thinking I shouldn't be alone. I'll be glad to have my life back when this is over." She peeled herself off the floor.

"Just remember," Jane said, "this our way of making sure you have a life when this is over."

"No one has any reason to want me dead. And we know who hit me now." Cerridwen knew better than to tell Jane that she was overreacting.

"As far as we know, they had no reason to want Mary dead either." Jane went back out into the hall, shutting the bathroom door behind her.

Cerridwen eyed the ceiling with distrust. *You never knew. With the way things were going the architecture could turn on her at any moment.* She reached for her phone.

Chapter 18

Thomas hated staff meetings. And this one was worse than usual. Some of the board members thought that one snow day necessitated an hour or more about how they were going to make up that day. Never mind how they were going to make up the time they were wasting now. Probably have a meeting about that as well. The joys of working at a private school.

His phone vibrated. He moved to shut it off and then stopped. It was a text form Cerridwen. He could tell it was Cerridwen because of the way she insisted on spelling everything correctly.

"Where are you?"

"Work. What's wrong?" He typed surreptitiously. He took the time to spell out all the words because he knew the abbreviations annoyed her. She didn't answer for a full minute. His fingers tensed around the phone. He was already looking for the exit when it gave another soundless wiggle.

"I need you."

Was it possible for your heart to speed up and stop at the same time? Ignoring the vice principal's freezing stare, he got up and walked out the door. She'd never liked him anyway. It was indicative of Thomas' feelings toward her that his inner sound track switched to the "Wicked Witch of the West" theme from the *Wizard of Oz* whenever the vice principal entered the room. It made for interesting listening when she and the head of the PTA were in the same room. Since that fateful night at the Loose Wheel, that particular parent was accompanied by Motley Crue's "Girls Girls Girls."

In the teacher's lounge, Thomas shrugged into his jacket and slapped his knit cap on his head.

"Where are you?" His fingers moved rapidly.

Her reply was quicker this time. "Whitmore."

What the hell was she doing there? And how fast could he get there? Fred was at work. Gerry had taken Teddy to a doctor's appointment. Thomas needed to get across town. It was another twenty minutes till the next bus, and then a half hour ride and at least ten minutes to get up the hill. Less if he ran. He had no idea how long he would have to wait for a cab.

"Is something wrong, Mr. Rakmelevich?" The tiny principal always made him feel like Gulliver among the Lilliputians. He felt guilty that her soundtrack leaned heavily on "The Lollipop Guild." But he had a soft spot for anyone who took the time to say his last name correctly.

"Family emergency. I need to leave." He waited tensely for her to demand more explanation. But whatever she saw when she craned her head back to look him in the face was enough.

"Go. You only have choir this afternoon. I can manage that. We'll get a sub for tomorrow if we have to." She let out an oof of surprise as he bent nearly double to hug her.

"Thank you."

He made it as far as the street before he remembered he didn't know how he was getting to Whitmore. He swore and turned to go back in the building almost colliding with Mrs. Gray as she came down the stairs. She settled the sherbet colored scarf around her shoulders Mrs. Gray, light of Victoria's society, president of the Historical Society and, as it turned out, board member of Frobisher Academy.

"Going somewhere, Mr. Rakmelevich?"

"Yes."

"You just missed the bus. Want a ride?"

How had he never noticed before what an angel this woman was?

"Yes, ma'am, I do."

"Where are you going?"

"Whitmore," he answered while trying to fold himself into the front seat. It was a little easier than normal because Mrs. Gray drove a Lincoln. She raised her eyebrows at his reply, but didn't comment.

Angel she might be, but she drove that Lincoln like a bat out of hell. They made it to Whitmore in just twenty minutes. There was an unmarked vehicle and a patrol car parked in the drive. Mrs. Gray blithely blocked them both in. An officer moved to tell her she couldn't park there. And Thomas walked right past him into the house.

"Thomas, what are you doing here?" Jane's eyebrows lifted.

"Cerridwen texted me. What is going on?"

"Did she now?" Jane's eyebrows tried to climb past her hairline. "Well, that would solve one problem. Joan has flipped her lid. Among other things she's admitted to attacking Cerridwen the night of the break-in. Cerridwen is understandably upset and I don't want her left alone, which was something else for her to be upset about. I had tried for Felix but I couldn't get a hold of him. At the same time we're trying to lay hands on Jason Witt to take charge of his mother. I'm leaning heavily in the direction of a psych evaluation. But that is neither here nor there. If you would…"

"I'm taking Cerridwen home with me. We'll be at Random House if you need us." By the time he had collected a worse-for-wear Cerridwen from the bathroom, Mrs. Gray had sailed in and taken charge of Joan. They were shut in the sun room with a female officer and a pot of tea, waiting for a doctor.

Thomas had moved into the old nursery at Random House which took up nearly half of the third floor at the rear of the house. As well as light and space, it had its own attached bathroom with an enormous tub. He could sit in it with his legs stretched out. There were very few places he could do that. It usually took the ancient boiler in the basement about five minutes to run hot, but it could fill the tub and then some with steamy water. He deposited Cerridwen in the bathroom with orders to get in the tub when it was full.

"There are towels under the sink," he called through the door. "And when you get out, there are tee shirts in the middle drawer of the dresser if you want something dry to wear. I'll be right back." After a moment he added "don't drown" as a precaution.

He took the stairs to the kitchen two at a time. The six flights were a lengthy trek even for his long legs. He needed comfort food. None of them drank tea, so there wasn't any in the house. He thought he would probably have to fix that at some point. In the meantime, he would have to substitute. Alcohol could be calming, couldn't it? He was rifling the cabinets when his phone rang. He had meant to turn it off. He recognized Felix's number, so he answered.

"I got a message from Jane saying I needed to come get Cerridwen and then another one saying never mind, you were there, and no explanation of either. What the hell is going on?" Felix projected perfect calm and blind with fury at the same time. *Hell of a trick that I must learn it someday*, Thomas thought. He always heard Felix's soundtrack as "Mars" from *The Planets*.

"Joan's broken with reality and confessed to all sorts of mayhem. Cerridwen is upset so I'm plying her with hot baths, vodka, chocolate, and old movies. Not necessarily in that order."

"Thomas, you romantic fool, how can she resist you? I'm in the middle of something, but I'll stop by later if I may. It might be late. I'm going to try and see if I can squeeze in throttling Joan."

"Take your time," Thomas said to the dead line. He made a detour to raid Teddy's DVDs. He called Fred at the Gargoyle and asked him to bring home dinner at end of shift. The lunch rush hadn't died down so this involved waiting on hold for several minutes. Then Jane called as he headed back to his room with the loot. He juggled the phone, the bottle, and the candy. He dropped the movies and had to grope for them on the stairs.

"How is she?" Jane did not believe in beating around the bush.

"Hang on, let me check." He kicked the door open and stopped dead. There in the middle of his California king, less than six feet from the door of the steamy bathroom, was Cerridwen curled up asleep in his Sevendust tee shirt. It was huge on her. A short sleeve on him came down past her elbow, and the hem fell well below the knee. "She's asleep."

"That's her usual reaction to stress. And right now probably for the best. Call me if you need me." Jane hung up.

Thomas dropped his burdens on the marble topped dresser. Throwing a blanket over Cerridwen, he settled into the mattress beside her. He took the side between her and the door more by instinct than anything else. He would just have to watch all those musicals without her.

She woke up three quarters of the way through "Silk Stockings." She rolled over and curled up against his side. She mumbled something into his shoulder about solid.

"What was that?" he asked.

She sighed and lifted her head. "I said, you are very solid."

"Well, I've been called worse things, I guess." *Not many that stung as much, though.*

"It was meant as a compliment."

"I'm sure it was. I'm just having a John Wayne moment." At least she hadn't said she thought of him like a brother. Anything but that. Friend you could work with, but there was no coming back from brother.

He offered her his drink and went to get the chocolate and another glass off the dresser.

"I said solid, not comfortable. What?" She grinned at his double take. "I liked Rio Lobo. Are girls not supposed to like John Wayne movies?" She took a sip of his drink and choked. "Dear God, what is in this?"

"Vodka and fruit juice. But mostly vodka. The juice is pretty much decorative. Chocolate?" He sat down on the edge of the bed and held the candy out to her.

"Please," she rasped. Maybe he should have put more juice in. She sat there for a moment looking at him with the glass in one hand and the chocolate in the other. He really should not be thinking what he was thinking. Not right now, anyway.

She stretched across him and set both objects on the crate that served as night table. He should do something about that. The unfinished wood looked odd against the green Chinese wallpaper.

And then Cerridwen kissed him and drove all thoughts of wallpaper out of his head. All thought entirely. His brain ceased to function. He lost himself in the feel and the taste of her. And then one lone thought struggled to the surface, gasping for air above the sea of hormones. He held her at arm's length, which put a good two and a half feet between them.

"Wait. Wait a minute." He couldn't believe he was saying this. Apparently neither could she.

"Why?"

"Line?" he croaked.

She frowned at him. "Well, I hadn't thought to write a script. Roleplay's not really my thing. But give me a sec, I'm sure I can come up with something."

"No, the line between friends and this." He waved one hand vaguely, still using the other to hold her off. He was not good with words right now. Her face brightened.

"Oh, that. Can we talk about it later?"

"No. You have to pick one side of the line or the other. Right now." Although he couldn't remember why if his life had depended on it.

"Why, for God sakes?"

Good question. Oh, hey, now Thomas remembered. "Because I love you." Shit, had he just blurted that out? He closed his eyes and waited for the roof to fall in.

"I love you, too," she said.

"Oh. Well, okay then." He wrapped his arms around her and fell back, pulling her with him. He wrapped one hand in her damp hair. The other hand found the hem of the tee shirt. There was a knock on the door.

"Fuck." He growled against her mouth. She laughed. "Shh. Don't move. If they can't hear us they might go away." They waited, pressed close together. There was another knock, followed by Teddy's voice.

"Thomas? That nice detective is here. He says can you come downstairs, please."

"I doubt very much he phrased it that way," he told Cerridwen. He raised his voice so Teddy could hear him. "Tell him I said no and to go away."

Teddy retreated. They had just enough time to find where they had left off before there was another knock.

"Who climbs stairs that fast?" Thomas wanted to know. Cerridwen was trying not to laugh. She was not successful.

"Mr. Rakmelevich. I need to speak to both of you. If you and Miss Evan-Jones could come downstairs." The voice of doom came through the door. Well, really the voice of Exposito, but at that moment it came to the same thing.

"I could learn to hate that man," Thomas said as Cerridwen tried to wiggle free. He gave up and let her go. "Tomorrow I am going to take a hammer to every doorbell and door handle in this godforsaken neighborhood. I will go stall Our Savior while you put some clothes on." He dragged himself up and out the door. Using his body to block the view through the opening, he shut it firmly behind him.

"Christ, would you go away?" Thomas asked in a conversational tone.

"We've been over this. My name is Jesús. It's not funny anymore. And no."

"Well, then she'll be out as soon as she remembers where her bra ended up." He smiled broadly.

Exposito glared at him. "It's not fair, you know. You get to be tall, and talented, and get the girl. It should at least be two out of three."

"Meanwhile, when's the last time you had to turn sideways to get through a door? You've never had to try and make a living with a degree in music. Or had to break up an oboe fight." Thomas shrugged him off and headed for the stairs. Exposito followed him.

"Mr. Rakmelevich." He stopped and took a deep breath. "Thomas, I wanted to tell you it was not your fault."

Thomas froze. "I don't know what you're talking about," he said, starting down the stairs again.

"I am not supposed to tell you this. So I didn't. But the ME found some kind of toxin in Hawkner's system. He thinks that's what killed her. He says either way she was dead before they packed her into the snow. Finding her sooner would not have helped." Exposito moved forward so he could look Thomas in the eyes, a feat he could accomplish standing several steps up. "It was not your fault. The only person to blame is the one that made her dead. Remember that." And then he took off down the stairs without looking back.

Chapter 19

Cerridwen woke to the sound of sirens. They were close and getting closer. It was rare that emergency vehicles came up the hill—less rare these days, but still not a regular occurrence.

Thomas unwound himself from her and the blankets, taking his body heat with him. She shivered in the cool air. He fumbled for the lamp as the sirens shot past the house at speed. The ambulance was going to Whitmore.

Thomas took off downstairs while she searched for her pants. She had got them on by the time he came back to look for his. "Fred went to see what's happening," he told her. "Gerry's getting dressed. Where is my shirt?"

Cerridwen cleared her throat and pointed to herself.

"Oh, yeah." He grinned. "Never mind, I'll wear another one."

They met Gerry and Teddy in the front hall as Fred came back in. Teddy had decided against getting dressed and was attired in an awe-inspiring dressing gown. Fred ignored this as normal and hardly noteworthy.

"Joan overdosed on sleeping pills. They're taking her to the hospital. Jason went with her. Mrs. Gray followed them. Stone is supposed to bring Jason's car. I told them we would meet them there. Jane's already on her way."

They all piled into Gerry's GTO for the frantic drive down the hill. It was a tight fit, made a little more awkward by Teddy still wearing his dressing gown.

Their arrival was pure chaos. Mrs. Gray soon straightened them out, sending them here and there on little errands. She settled Teddy by simply telling him to sit down and be quiet. It helped that he had the reactions of bystanders to entertain him. An old man in a blue and gold dressing gown was not what one thought to see in the emergency room at two a.m.

However, her powers came to naught on the Sand sisters who had arrived shortly after the rest. Unlike Teddy, they had taken the time to get dressed. Pearl never appeared in public in the all-together. Ruby never appeared in the all-together for less than a couple of grand. They simply ignored Mrs. Gray and set to people watching, commenting on what they observed and even engaging their subjects in conversation. A few people moved in an effort to get away from them, but most soon realized that this was futile.

With the organizing out of the way, Mrs. Gray seemed to deflate, sinking in on herself with a sigh. Fred and Gerry came back with coffee that no one drank. A little while later, Thomas arrived with sandwiches that nobody ate. There was nothing left to do, but wait.

Stone showed up with the Witts' car and some things for Jason who would stay the night, what was left of it, with his mother. Exhausted, he dropped into the chair beside Mrs. Gray.

"I should have paid more attention," Mrs. Gray said into the silencc. "I should have watched her more carefully." She trailed off, her hands shaking.

"I don't understand why she would do this." Stone shook his head. "It seems so unlike her."

"It does seem strange for someone with such a reverence for life." Fred swirled his unwanted coffee in its Styrofoam cup. "To stand up for the rights of a tree but not yourself. It's off somehow."

"Don't you have to be somewhat off, though?" Gerry asked. "Suicide is hardly a reasonable solution."

"Maybe it wasn't on purpose. She was upset. Maybe she just made a mistake." Teddy left off flirting with a passing nurse long enough to throw in his two cents.

"Do you think it had something to do with Hawkner's death?" Stone asked. They all thought about this for a moment.

"Do you think Joan had something to do with Ann's death?" Mrs. Gray's hands shook as she set her cup on the low table beside her. "You think this incident was prompted by guilt?"

Stone opened his mouth, but any reply he would have made was lost.

Jason, coming to report on his mother's condition, had heard her question. "Are you implying that my mother is guilty of both attempted suicide and murder?" His low tone and blank expression were more disturbing than any outburst.

The remaining color drained from Mrs. Gray's face. Her usual unshakable calm crumbled. She shook her head. "No, of course not. I was just thinking out loud."

"Yes, I heard what you thought. You might consider just how unlikely it is that an eleven year old child committed murder and stuffed the victim in a tree, unaided. You might instead think about the other people around at the time. Other *older* people." The ice in his voice was more than sufficient to lower the temperature in the room. He turned away from her and addressed the others as if she no longer existed. "They're pumping Mom's stomach now. Then they are going to keep her for observation while they run some tests. They're checking for kidney damage and possible brain damage. There may be a chance of hemorrhaging." Quiet fury poured off of him in waves as he left them. Mrs. Gray went after him.

Stone hesitated. He rose as if to follow them, but then thought better of it. "Better to let them work it out," he muttered half to himself.

Better to stay out of the crossfire, thought Cerridwen.

Teddy had been watching the proceedings with rapt attention. "Who was that?" he asked Cerridwen.

"Who, Jason?" *Was Teddy about to have one of his "spells?"* she wondered. He often had one when he felt he wasn't getting enough attention, turning his so-called dementia on and off to suit himself.

"No." He shook his head. "The other one. The woman."

"That's Mrs. Gray," Thomas answered. "She's on the board at my school."

"She's also current president of the Historical Society and chairperson of about a dozen charities," Cerridwen expanded.

This struck Teddy as funny. "No, really. She never. Oh, that is funny. Do you know who that is?" Teddy was bouncing with suppressed glee. Cerridwen just shook her head. Teddy was laughing out loud now.

"That, my dear, is Lilith."

It took her a moment to remember their earlier conversation. It had been more than a week. Understanding dawned. "No!" It was hard to believe. "Lilith from Witt's 'community of souls?' That Lilith?"

"The very same," confirmed Teddy. "It's true. The staid Mrs. Gray is Topless Lilith."

Fred choked on his coffee. Thomas was uncharacteristically wide-eyed. Stone came to point as he did whenever Witt or his disciples were mentioned.

"The mind boggles," was Gerry's opinion.

"Well, you have to picture everything higher. And not so wrinkly."

"I am trying very hard not to picture it," Thomas said with his hands over his face.

"Well, all I have to say is your loss. You should ask Thorn if he has any pictures." Teddy scratched his chin. "Mrs. Gray, you said. Gray, Gray. I know that name. Well, I'll be," he said after a moment. "Topless Lilith married Toad. That's unexpected, I must say."

Cerridwen wanted to ask who Toad was. She had a vague memory of Teddy referring to him under the crabapple, but she wasn't sure.

"Well that is odd," put in Pearl. "When they first met she wouldn't give him the time of day. Which I never understood. Seemed like a nice boy."

"He wasn't of her class, don't you know," Ruby supplied. "She came from old money. Or as old as it gets on this coast. Jumped up robber barons fancying themselves the new royalty. Course, things changed in a hurry when her Daddy landed them in financial ruin."

"Strange that someone living in a commune would be classist," chimed in Stone. "Didn't Mr. Gray pass away recently?"

"If you call sometime last year recent," Ruby said, shrugging.

Before they could go into detail, the outer doors opened. Jane strode in with Exposito close behind. They blew past reception, ignoring the group huddled in the waiting area, and cornered a doctor. Cerridwen recognized him as Blue Scrubs, her nemesis from her earlier visit.

Blue Scrubs caught sight of her and did a double take. He took in her escort, his eyes widening when they touched on Teddy. He took a step back towards the swing doors, gesturing for the two detectives to follow him.

"That's done it," Fred told her. "You've given the man a phobia."

"I didn't give him anything. I was unconscious. It was you people that put the fear of God into him."

"What do you mean 'you people?'" Fred raised an eyebrow.

"Shut up, Tonto." Cerridwen waved a hand at him in dismissal. He just laughed at her. "You know what I think?" she said after a moment. "I think he did it."

"Who did what?" Gerry turned sideways and tried to curl up on a row of plastic chairs. He kicked Stone in the process, almost knocking him out of his seat. Not entirely on accident.

"That Blue Scrubs, the doctor. I think he killed Ann. Think about it. He keeps turning up, but plot wise he has no reason to be here. Besides, he's acting all shifty for no reason. Look at him. He's practically a walking Chekhov's gun."

"Chekhov didn't have a gun, he had a phaser." Gerry opened one eye and peered at her.

"Chekhov the Russian playwright," Stone corrected, shoved Gerry's feet aside and reclaimed part of his seat. "He said if you mentioned a gun in the first act you had to fire it in third. If this was a story, having mentioned him twice we would have to make use of him somehow."

"But why would Blue Scrubs want to kill Ann Hawkner? Damn, one of us has to find out his name," Fred said.

"The Historical Society acquired his home by unscrupulous means and he wants it back," offered Pearl.

"No," Ruby disagreed. "The holier-than-thou -society demolished his home to make way for more museum parking."

It took the others a moment to understand the game. Stone caught on quickly. "He is compelled to kill middle aged female historians because they remind him of the history professor that broke his young, freshman heart," he put in.

"Oh, good one!" said Pearl. "Worthy of Felix. Your turn, Cerridwen."

"Well, off the top of my head? He's Mary Paul's long lost something-or-other. And he's seeking revenge by killing off one by one the people he thinks are responsible her death."

Stone choked on his coffee, which must have been cold by now. Fred just shook his head. The humor, black as it was, relieved the tension for a moment.

Cerridwen had warmed to her idea and would have expanded on it, but Jane emerged from the swinging doors and beckoned her. She was in professional mode. Only someone who knew her well could tell how shaken she was.

"Someone tried to kill Joan." Jane stated without preamble.

"How can you be certain it wasn't an accident?"

"There were two doses. The first was the prescribed dose of the sleeping pills she was given this afternoon. The second dose was given later. It hadn't completely dissolved yet. And, according to the doctor, it was massive. He thinks it unlikely that she would have been awake enough after the second dose to take it herself. It is also a different medication than the one she was prescribed."

"Do they know when she was given the second dose?" Cerridwen asked. They were both thinking the same thing. When would have a definite effect on who.

"They are working on it. The possibilities are limited. They can't do anything more for her tonight. And neither can we. Don't go anywhere alone. Stay with Thomas until I get home."

"And just what is Thomas going to do if someone tries to poison me?" Cerridwen had to ask. "Intimidate the poison?"

"Hopefully he would scare them off before they had a chance to poison you. Go home. Make sure to take Teddy with you. He's making the natives nervous." She started back down the hall with a sigh.

"Oh, Jane!" Cerridwen caught her arm. "Teddy says Mrs. Gray is topless Lilith from Witt's commune."

Jane laughed in surprise. "Well, that's news. How did that come about?"

"According to Teddy she married that guy they all called Toad for some reason. She might be a source of information."

"I know where this is going. And I would tell you no if I thought it would do any good. So here is what I'm going to do." Jane held up a hand to silence Cerridwen, who was about to say she didn't know what Jane was talking about. "Ask questions in a casual way. Nothing pointed." She jabbed a finger at her. "And you tell me everything."

"If I find out anything," Cerridwen capitulated.

"No if. Everything she says you report to me. I'll see you in the morning after I wrap up this circus."

Cerridwen saw her sooner than that. When they pulled into the driveway of Random House they could clearly see the wall that cut Whitmore off from the rest of the court. They had an unobstructed view of the six foot high letters sprawled across its length. The bright red paint demanded to know, "Where did Mary go?"

Teddy merely shrugged and shuffled towards the house. Thomas made an exasperated noise and banged his head against the roof of the GTO. Gerry and Fred played rock paper scissors for who got to call Jane with the news. And Cerridwen decided she had had enough and just went to bed.

Chapter 20

The late morning sun woke Cerridwen. She eyed the unfamiliar wallpaper distrustfully till she remembered where she was. She had not had the energy to take in her surroundings yesterday. She sat up and stretched, dislodging a sleeping Thomas. He grumbled and spread out to take up more of the bed.

Thomas had taken a very linear approach to decorating. The bed was shoved against the wall by the bathroom with a carved and very beautiful, expense antique Balinese screen as a headboard. A baroque, marble-topped dresser was grudgingly shoved as far into the corner as it would go. The length of the room, both the inner wall and the space under the windows, was taken up with assorted instruments and components of what appeared to be at least five stereos wired together. The opposite wall of the long room was filled with floor to ceiling diagonal shelving holding the largest collection of vinyl records she had ever seen. They barely avoided blocking the tiny door to the room next door.

"I wonder what he did with the Nanny's room," she thought out loud, eyeing the little door.

"It has all my recording equipment," Thomas mumbled into her shoulder, foiling her efforts to disentangle herself from the blankets.

"I would have made it a closet." She shoved at him with no discernible effect.

"I don't have that many clothes." He shrugged.

The man had warped priorities. She slapped his wandering hands and eeled out of the bad. "Bookshelves, then. Aren't you supposed to be torturing children at tuba point?"

"I don't teach tuba. The principal called and said I could take time off till Monday for my family emergency." He abandoned his pursuit and flopped across the mattress.

"She lets you take off a lot of time for a new employee."

"I have very impressive credentials. And I'm pretty. Why are you getting dressed?"

"I need to go home. I want my own clothes. And I have to meet the locksmith. And I have work to get done."

"That's a lot of reasons for going. I can think of one reason to stay." He wiggled his eyebrows suggestively.

"I'm sure you can." Cerridwen went into the bathroom to look for her sweater.

"We have slept together twice, three times if you count last night and this morning separately. But we haven't done anything other than sleep," he called after her.

"That's not true. We've watched three movies. And don't forget the time I threw up on you." She called through the open door.

"And they say romance is dead. Still not quite what I had in mind. Not something I want to repeat either, if I had to be honest."

Cerridwen emerged from the bathroom with an incredulous expression. "The body count is at two. Depending on Joan's progress, it may well be three. And what you're complaining about is that you're not getting laid?" She pulled at her mangled sweater, dry but obviously the worse for wear. "Would it be tactless, do you think, to tell Joan she owes me a vintage sweater?"

"It might not be the right time to bring it up. And I will not say anything about your messed up priorities. Of course I'm coming with you." He heaved himself out of the bed.

"I wonder what Mrs. Gray is up to today." Cerridwen's voice was muffled as she searched for her shoes under the bed. "I want to talk to her. All I got out of her last night was that she had indeed married Toad, and that she hated that nickname. She felt it was unkind and that his eyes didn't protrude that much."

Thomas stuck his head out of the bathroom. "Does Jane know you're questioning people?"

"Jane said she wouldn't tell me no, because she knew it wouldn't work. Which is almost the same thing as permission. Are you coming?" His answer was not clear. She suspected it wasn't flattering either, but she let it go.

In the end, Thomas and Fred both went with her, trailing Teddy like an easily amused balloon. She left them in the kitchen and shut the door to her office. As recently as week ago, she would not have left them unsupervised. Now she just didn't care.

Cerridwen rewrote chapter twenty-two three times and was still unhappy with it before the doorbell demanded attention. She went to answer it with equal parts relief and irritation. As she passed through the kitchen she saw Thomas and Teddy playing a card game that somehow involved the chess board from the library and the salt and pepper shakers. Fred seemed to be squaring off to do battle with the ancient Aga range. Something loud, very metal, and possibly German blared on Fred's laptop. She had to raise her voice when she took a moment to remind them that the chess board and the stove were both antiques before going to let Carl the locksmith in.

"Them biddies at the Historical Society were on the phone first thing this morning. The wanted me to know I'm violating a historic landmark." He grinned at her. "I said lady, that house and I don't have that kind of relationship. There is no truth to the rumors, we are just good friends." He laughed at his own joke.

Cerridwen couldn't help grinning back. "Your relationship or lack thereof with my house is none of their business. And I will tell them that." She left Carl dismantling the hardware on the front door and went back to her office.

The call to the Historical Society only produced a confused secretary, who had no idea who Cerridwen was or why her locks were a problem. Next she made a call to the lawyer that administered the day to day matters of her grandmother's trust. One of the attorney's minions promised to send the Historical Society a politely worded letter explaining why the locks were being changed, and also, why it was none of their business. It was not the first time they had to do this. The Historical Society had to be gently reminded of its boundaries.

Maybe that was why it took so long for the question to finally occur to her. She stomped back through the kitchen, past the ever-evolving card game, which now involve her calendar in an unknown capacity, down the length of the house, back to the front door.

"How did the biddies know?" Cerridwen asked.

Carl didn't look up from the unidentifiable piece of front door he was holding. "How did they know what?" He was not giving her his full attention.

"How did the biddies from the Historical Society know that I was having the locks changed? I didn't tell them. I assume you didn't call them and announce you intended to violate my house. So how did they know?"

"Don't know. Saw the truck maybe. That detective anywhere around?" Carl still hadn't looked up from the bit of metal. He ran his finger over it, chewing his lip.

"Jane? Upstairs asleep, I think. Why?"

"You might want to go wake her up. And tell her that your front door has had its lock picked." He held the lock's innards out to her. "See where the face of the tumbler pins are all scratched up?"

"Those are not just the scratches that you get on a door from keys and what not? It is an old door."

Carl shook his head. "If they were on the face plate maybe. But not on the inside. You get those scratches from something that hasn't been cut to fit the way the key was. See?" He pointed.

No, she didn't see. Cerridwen wasn't even sure what she was looking at. But it certainly lent credence to Joan's insistence that someone else had been in the house the night she had hit Cerridwen.

Of course she would tell Jane. But Jane had been awake all night. And it wasn't as if she could do anything about it now. Besides, Cerridwen had something else she wanted to do first. She had to go upstairs to find shoes. Her ancestors had assumed that she would have someone to fetch and carry and therefore would not need a conveniently placed hall closet.

"Yahtzee!" yelled Teddy as she came down the stairs.

"Gin," countered Thomas. "And I take your queen."

"No, you don't. Double sixes! And a bottle of ranch dressing." Teddy cackled.

"Where the hell did the dice come from?" Their voices faded as she ran down the curved front steps, through the front garden and out on to the sidewalk. To her left, past Random House, garish red letters still bled from the surface of Whitmore's outer wall. She didn't cross the street but followed the gentle downhill arc of the pavement to the right, towards the Gate House near the entrance to the Court.

The snow and slush had melted, leaving everything gray and soggy. The surviving vegetation was limp and dripping. Cerridwen splashed through a puddle as she crossed where the avenue intersected the court. Standing in the drive to Gate House she could not see her own house clearly. The view of Witt's End was blocked by its own garden wall at one end and the looming Green Man Tree at the other. The door to the conservatory was at the back of the house and not visible from the street at any angle. She could see Carl's van on the street, but last time he had parked in the service lane that ran along the side of the house, the side opposite from where she was now standing.

Turning to eye Gate House and then the empty street with equal distrust, Cerridwen picked her way through the mud and slush of the gravel drive. The view from the portico was even more limited. Ann Hawkner could not have seen Carl the locksmith from her house. The tall trees were likely to have blocked the line of sight from the upper floor as well. She drew the line at breaking in to check. She didn't want to put Jane to the embarrassment of having to arrest her. On the other hand, Jane was Homicide. Maybe she would get arrested by an officer she hadn't met yet. That would be a fun way to meet new friends.

"What are you doing?" Fred's quite voice made her jump nearly out of her skin. Studying the house in front of her, she had not seen him come across the street.

"Damnit, Silverheels, stop sneaking up on me. The Historical Society is upset that I am having my historic locks changed," she began.

"How did they know that you're having the locks changed?" Fred's eyes narrowed. Against the thought or the slanting sunlight? Both, maybe. The nickname he just ignored.

"The logical answer would be that they heard it from Hawkner. She was a member. And their resident spy. I still have a message from her on machine from her about it. I didn't get it till after she was dead." She shivered slightly as she replayed the message in her head. "What I can't figure out is how she found out."

"Hawkner couldn't see it from her house. And you didn't tell her?" Fred thought out loud.

"I never talked to the woman more than I could help. She left a nasty taste in my mouth. I certainly didn't natter on about my personal life. She could have found out if she tried to use a key. The only key that I know is out there is the one Joan had."

"The one Joan lost the night of the break-in. The key that might have been picked up by the person she said interrupted her. The one she mistook you for." Fred followed her to the logical conclusion. Cerridwen rubbed the spot where the candlestick had hit the back of her head. It was becoming a habit. They stood there in silence contemplating the reach of the Historical Society before an unrelated thought occurred to Cerridwen.

"You haven't blown up my stove, have you?"

"Nah. I've cooked on worse. Or should I say older? I came to tell you breakfast is ready. Carl said you disappeared out the front door.

I thought I should find out if you had actually disappeared before I gave Thomas a heart attack." Fred shrugged.

"Teddy is the one his nineties," she pointed out as they started back to her house, picking their way through the mud and jumping over the worse spots.

"Yeah, but nothing fazes Teddy. Except woman with agile minds. Whatever he means by that."

"It's better not to ask. He will tell you." Cerridwen knew this from bitter experience. Fred just laughed.

Someone had decided the news about the lock was worth waking Jane up for. Cerridwen could see her roommate through the open front door, still in her pajamas, her cell phone pressed to her ear.

Chapter 21

Jane had been reluctant to go to work and leave Cerridwen alone in the house. “This place has become Grand Central Station, but when I need one of them there is not a warm body to be found,” Jane groused.

“That’s a bit of a cliché. Maybe you could say it’s a veritable crossroads. Or that our population density has risen sharply. Oh, hey, I know. We’re Ellis Island, gateway to the West coast. Well, really gateway to my library. But you know what I mean,” Cerridwen said.

“We are under siege by robbers and murders and you’re bitching about my awkward metaphors?” Jane demanded.

“Not bitching. Critiquing.”

“Seriously?”

Cerridwen didn’t answer, deciding from Jane’s tone that discretion was the better part of safety. She thought “A warm body could not be had for love or money” would be more elegant, but Jane might feel the implication of prostitution was inappropriate.

Jane gave her a hard, narrowed-eyed look. "Do me a favor, critique with the doors locked and keep the phone handy. I am well aware that everybody and his brother has keys to this place, but it might at least slow them down."

With Jane gone, Cerridwen turned the music up and the phone off. She sorted out a problem with her timeline. This was not the sort of book where people had conversations after they were dead. She renumbered chapters and settled down to wrestle with her ending.

Her villain had just escaped arrest, only to die in a fiery car crash on his way to the airport and parts unknown. It gave the hostility and anger of the integration scene a place to lead. And after months of battling an uncooperative Hal Norland, burning him to ash and cinder relieved her frustration nicely.

Gloating over his heated end, she took the phone into the kitchen with her to find something to eat. The last of the cookies and a can of Coke accompanied her out in to the hall. The late hour cast the house in shadow. Cerridwen didn't bother turning on the lights, as she was only passing through on her way to the bedroom and would only have to turn them off again.

The crack of light under the library door was a bright slash across the darkness. There was no reason for the light to be on, or the door to be shut. Cerridwen listened but couldn't pick up any sound. She moved back into the kitchen and called Jane's number. It went straight to voice mail. A call to her office reached a harassed sounding desk sergeant who said Jane was on a call and to try her cell phone. Cerridwen thanked him and hung up without telling him she had called the cell already.

"If I do wait for Jane, and she ditches work to come haring back here to find nothing, I will feel a real fool." After a moment's thought, she tiptoed to the door and listened hard. No sound was forthcoming.

She turned the well-oiled handle with only a whisper from the latch and peered through the narrowest possible opening. What she could see of the room was empty. She eased the door another inch or so and gained a wider view. Still the room appeared empty.

The shelves were disarranged. A few volumes had tumbled to the floor. One lost the battle with gravity as she watched it. Irritation gave way to rage as her eye caught the sparkle of broken glass. With all the keys floating around, it was hardly necessary to shatter one of her historic sash windows to gain entry. Maybe conducted tours would cut down on the traffic. What the hell, maybe an open house. She could advertise. *Come and search my library at your leisure.*

She moved to secure the blowing drapes. The breeze had the cold, damp taste of rain. There was the faintest of sounds from behind the door. It was all the warning Cerridwen needed. Grabbing the handle, she threw all her weight against the wood, driving the door into the body behind it. The cookies crunched as the box hit the floor. The can of Coke rolled unheeded under the table. There was a grunt and a thump as the person was pushed hard against the wall. A disembodied hand scrambled for a grip on the edge of the door. A small scar, old and badly healed, shown pale against the inner wrist.

With a silent apology to the plaster work, she held on tight and slammed the thick wood home twice more before the other person gained traction. The door swung back hard. It hit her in the shoulder and shoved her backwards into the hall. She lost her grip and fell, skidding a little on the stone, temporarily blind in the relative darkness. From the sound of it, her intruder was making a hasty exit through the broken window.

She swore at length with imagination and a rich vocabulary. As she picked herself up, she had no doubt she would have painful memories in the morning.

The phone rang. She retrieved it from under the console table and answered it as she lay on the floor in the cool darkness.

"Hi, Jane. I just did something stupid."

Of course, Jane was mad. There was no getting around that. Exposito was unsympathetic. The window guy refused to come until the morning. And, to top it all off, the cookies were so many crumbs. A uniformed officer had taken charge of them and the large, wet footprint on the package.

It seemed when your cop roommate wouldn't answer her phone you were supposed to take the back stairs and lock yourself in your bedroom, then call 911. When Cerridwen assured Jane she would remember that next time, Jane growled in response. Into the middle of this marched Ruby, brandishing a croquet mallet. Teddy was close behind her with a steel-spined umbrella. The cloud of alcohol fumes indicated they were on their way home from a garden club meeting.

"We saw the lights, dear." Ruby eyed Exposito appreciatively. "Is there anyone, I mean, anything we can do?"

"Yes," Jane said. "Since you're here, you can babysit Cerridwen. Or better yet, you can babysit each other. Until this mess is over, I don't want anyone going anywhere alone. It's the buddy system from here on out."

Cerridwen refrained from pointing out she hadn't actually gone anywhere.

"What on earth were you doing alone in the house?" Teddy twirled his umbrella.

"I live here," Cerridwen pointed out.

"Yes, I know. It was the alone part I was getting at." He and Ruby followed her into the salon.

"Jane had to work. And I can't expect the rest of you to put your lives on hold indefinitely. Felix still has a house guest, you had your meeting. It would be just a little unreasonable to put that kind of pressure on Joan right now. And God knows that Jason has enough on his plate right now. Besides, who's to say another person here would have made a difference one way or the other?" Cerridwen dropped on to the settee with a sigh.

Ruby plopped into a chair with the mallet across her knees. Teddy propped his umbrella against the fireplace surround.

"What I meant to say," Teddy spoke with exaggerated patience. "Is where is Thomas?"

"He had a work thing. He's going to catch a ride home with Fred and Gerry later."

"You didn't call him? And how do you think he's going to feel about that when he finds out?"

"I couldn't ask him to blow off work again. He's already taken enough time off because of me. Even if…" She trailed off. It sounded weak even to her. The problem was saying it out loud. Everything sounded better in her head, but then, wasn't that always the way?

“Even if what? Even if you’re in a relationship? Because that's what it is, and you owe it to that boy as well as yourself to take it seriously. It’s not fair to either of you to not to.” Teddy was wearing a stern expression. It did not sit comfortably on his usually cheerful face.

“I know that.” The irritation gave Cerridwen’s voice a sharp edge.

“So what is the problem?” Teddy’s voice was just as sharp. Ruby was uncharacteristically silent, but she watched with the air of someone prepared to be entertained.

“To start with, he‘s nearly half a decade younger than me.” She hated that she sounded so defensive.

“Five years.” Teddy snorted. “What’s that to anything? It has no bearing on his character. And I would hope it has no bearing on how you feel about him. And those should be the only two factors under consideration.”

“I have a hard time shaking the feeling I’m in a Jackie Collins novel.”

“And what’s that to anything when it’s at home? Ms. Collins has a steady income and by all accounts two happy marriages under her belt. And there is something to be said for both.

“Marriage number one ended in divorce,” Cerridwen pointed out.

“And what is that to anything? You might get divorced so you won’t date the boy? That is cart before the horse if I ever heard it.”

“Oh, God. Teddy darling, I love you like the grandfather I never met, but I am not discussing this with you. It’s just too surreal.”

“Bullshit. You just don’t want to argue with me because you know I’ll win. Because I’m right.”

“I don’t have a history of making good decisions in that department,” she hedged.

“So you made one mistake. That’s not all that bad a record in this day and age, all things considered. I have two divorces to my name. God knows how many mistakes Ruby over there has made. It hardly seems fair to punish him for someone else’s bad behavior.”

"I'm not punishing him. I'm just having difficulty trusting my judgment."

"Have you slept with him yet?" Ruby entered the conversation with all the grace of tanker wallowing its way into a shallow port.

"Ruby! What the hell?" Cerridwen found, for a wonder, that she did have boundaries.

"I think you should. For science! Or the very least for curiosity's sake. Or my curiosity anyways. Any way you look at it," Ruby stabbed a finger at her. "You owe it to womankind."

"Just how much did she have to drink, exactly?"

"She has a point." Thomas stood in the doorway, arms wide and a bag of takeout in either hand. "I mean, look at me."

"I got to agree." Gerry brushed past him carrying a two twelve packs of beer. "At first I didn't think it was a good idea. But he is pretty dishy. And he has a steady job. Girls are supposed to be into that kind of thing." He set down the booze and made room for Fred on the sofa.

Cerridwen groaned and dropped her head in her hands. "Just how much of that conversation did you hear?" She didn't really want to know but had to ask.

"Oh, just about all of it. I didn't catch why you should have called me." Thomas set the food on the low table. Cerridwen's relief lasted all of three seconds.

"She had another break-in. Ruby and I think that she should have called you when it happened." Teddy ignored her frantic shushing.

"Speak for yourself," Ruby countered. "All I said was she should sleep with him. Fred dear, hand me one of those beers."

Thomas went still for a beat. His knuckles went white against the Styrofoam container. His hands unclenched with visible effort. "I'm going to get plates." He turned and walked out of the room.

Ruby broke the tense silence. "Bring some forks, too," she called after him.

"Are you willfully oblivious?" Fred asked.

"Of course not. I'm just so old I don't give a shit." Ruby shrugged.

Teddy stared hard at Cerridwen. He didn't have to say anything to get his point across. She had a mess to clean up and it was nobody's fault but her own. She followed Thomas to the kitchen and watched from the doorway as he gathered plates and utensils. His abrupt movements had an unfamiliar tightness.

"I don't think I've ever seen you mad before," she said.

"I'm not mad," he growled.

"No, you're furious," she agreed.

He set the stack of plates on the table between them with exaggerated care. "I'm not mad at you. I'm mad at the situation. I'm upset that things like this keep happening and there doesn't seem to be any way to protect you from it short of locking down the neighborhood and taking away all your freedom. I'm unhappy that you didn't call when you needed me. But mostly I'm pissed at myself."

"Well, that's a little unreasonable. I think you're the only one around here who hasn't done something to piss anyone off. Are you feeling left out?" Her attempt to lighten the mood fell so flat it made a thump as it hit the floor.

"I'm pissed at myself because somewhere along the way I did something to make you feel you couldn't call me. Either that or Teddy's right and you don't think this is serious." Other people's voices rose when they were upset. Thomas's voice got quieter and deeper. It was the more unsettling of the two options.

"I wouldn't take anything Teddy said too seriously. He just came from a garden club meeting so he's drunk. Plus, he's crazy." Nerves made Cerridwen flippant. She knew almost immediately that it was the wrong thing to say. He lifted an eyebrow and waited.

"I didn't call because I hadn't had time to think about it."

"You called Teddy."

"No, I did not. They just showed up. They were on their way home and wandered in, as they do most days. Everything happened very fast. There were the cops and then there was Ruby hitting on the cops. And Jane was already pissed at me for being dumb. And when I did have time to think about it, it didn't seem fair to call you."

"That doesn't even make sense." He threw his hands up. For the first time, his voice rose.

"Doesn't it? We've know each other less than a month and look at how much I've already messed with your life. How many times have you left work or not even gone because of me? How many times have you changed your plans? How many times have you gone without sleep? Hell, half the time you don't even get a chance to go home." She was tired and frustrated. She hated that she had to concentrate not to cry.

"It doesn't matter. I love you. And you take care of the people you love. I thought you understood that. Even if I do make you feel like Jackie Collins." He was still pissed, but there was a tiny hint of amusement there as well.

"Oh, God. You really did hear everything." She rubbed a hand across her tired eyes.

"Pretty much." He put his arms around her and rested his chin on her head.

"For the record, I said I felt like I was in a Jackie Collins novel. Slight difference."

"Noted."

"Were you really mad?" Her voice was muffled against the front of his shirt.

"Scared. That I'd done something between now and the last time to make you think you couldn't call me when you needed to. Or that Teddy was right and you didn't take me seriously. Trust me, I am very aware of the age difference. I know it puts me at a disadvantage. I figured it would be an uphill battle. I just didn't think I would fuck up that quickly." His arms tightened around her. She squeezed back.

"You didn't fuck up. I just hadn't had time to react. I was lying on Joan's bathroom floor for about twenty minutes before I called you last time."

"This is supposed to make me feel better?" Thomas asked the ceiling.

"I was trying to explain that I do take you and this relationship seriously. But if you're going to be flippant, never mind." She pushed away from him. He pulled her back. By the time they went back to the salon, everyone had left, taking most of the food and all of the beer with them. But by that point, neither of them cared.

Chapter 22

Jane came home in the morning. She was pleased that Thomas had stayed the night. She suggested, or rather insisted, that he continue to do so.

"Until the locks are changed, and the Hysterical Society be damned, there has to be at least one other person in the house at all times."

"If you count the intruders, I'm really never alone," Cerridwen pointed it out. Jane did not think this was funny. Cerridwen surrendered to the inevitable. She was now ranked above "make sure Teddy is wearing pants" on the list of priorities.

The end result, Cerridwen was once again surrounded by a rotation of Thomas, his roommates, and the occasional Sand sister. She wanted to know what Ruby or Pearl was supposed to do against an intruder but was afraid to ask. She had come downstairs this afternoon to find Fred and Carl the locksmith around her kitchen table as if they lived there.

It wouldn't do any good to go somewhere else either. They simply followed her en mass. She settled for shutting her office door. She emerged briefly to deal with the window guy. He knew Carl the locksmith and seemed inclined to stay. She really didn't give a damn at this point. They could have a party if they wanted as long her window got fixed.

She was tired, sore, and pissed off that her house had been invaded again. But more than that, she was scared. After a lifetime of relative safety, she had been attacked twice in her own home in less than a month. When Fred came to tell her lunch was ready, she looked around for something to throw at the interloper, but then thought better of it. He had cooked, after all. There was no reason to shoot herself in the foot. She hit save and closed her laptop.

When she emerged, she found Carl and the window guy had been joined by Thorn. He wanted to confide something to her, she could tell. He had that look in his eye that people got when they wanted to make their problems her problems. He felt it was vitally important to tell her whatever it was. Why did people do that? It wasn't like there weren't other options. She had a resident homicide detective, for Christ sake. What more did people want from her? Thorn looked older folded into the chair near the window. He didn't look at her, instead looking out over the damp, bare garden.

"Felix says that Joan tried to commit suicide." His voice was strained. He sounded tired.

"They're not sure it was suicide. She had more than one dose of sleeping pills in her. The doctor believes they were taken at two different times. It is possible that someone slipped her the second dose." Cerridwen hesitated to tell him, but he was so obviously upset.

"That boy, Thomas, I think his name is." Thorn sighed. "He told Felix that Joan found Mary's stuff. That that is what upset her."

"It certainly didn't seem to help. But she was already upset. If it hadn't been that, it would been something else." Cerridwen tried to reassure him. If he felt better maybe he would go away. If he didn't leave soon, she would abandon him to the tender mercies of Fred and the bottle of vodka he had produced out of thin air. If they were going to insist on taking up space, they could at least serve a purpose.

"I still picture Joan as a little girl. Seeing her like this is hard." He twisted his fingers in a gesture oddly like Joan's habit. Cerridwen's better nature warred with her desire to meet her deadline. She wondered if she could go back to work without him noticing. Maybe he would just drone on quietly in the corner.

"It's unsettling to think I caused her distress. I meant it for the best."

That caught her attention. "How could you be responsible?"

"I left Mary's stuff there. I didn't know what else to do. One day Mary was gone. And everybody said she had left for one reason or another. But all her stuff was there. It seemed wrong to pack it up. And I figured it was only a matter of time before it occurred to one of those leeches to pocket some or all of it. I assumed she would come back at some point. And I didn't know where to send it, or to who. So I put some stuff in boxes and I locked up her room. It was supposed to be temporary. And then I suppose I forgot about it. I never thought it was still there." Thorn absently tried to pull his right thumb off his hand.

Well, this was a can of worms. Why couldn't people unburden themselves to Jane who could actually do something about it? Or at least pick a time when she was within shouting distance? It wasn't as if Cerridwen could actually do anything for them. And they only had to repeat everything again. All these confiding people added to the process was just more trouble.

"I thought maybe Mary was avoiding me. I had a thing for her. It was probably painfully obvious. She was so smart, so competent. But she didn't feel the same way. I think she thought I was too young. If I thought that Joan would have found that stuff, if I thought it mattered, I would have put them anywhere else."

Cerriudwen couldn't help but notice that even now Thorn couldn't imagine a scenario where he wasn't a major player. Whatever had happened to Mary and subsequently Joan had to be because of him in some way. Were all people this self-absorbed? She wondered if it was human nature. Did they all see themselves as the main character?

"Avoiding you couldn't be the only reason she would have had for leaving?" Cerridwen couldn't help asking. She sent a silent apology in Jane's direction. But it wasn't really sticking your nose in when people battered down your door. "You don't walk away from your job and all your possessions just because someone annoys you." It was possible that he had done more than annoyed Mary Paul. You might leave everything to get away from a stalker.

"There was something strange going on between her and Toad," he offered after some thought. He pulled on his thumb and then rubbed his wrist under the cuff of his sleeve. "But I couldn't tell you what it was about. And by the end of the summer, Mary was gone and Lilith and Toad were a couple. Which was a surprise to one and all." Thorn frowned at the wet plantings outside the window.

"Mary and Toad were a couple?" That went against what Cerridwen knew from her grandmother's journal. Constance Frey had believed her friend to be "unattached."

"No, I don't think that it was sex with Toad and Mary. They didn't act like they were attracted, either of them." Thorn gave some thought before shaking his head. "But there was some kind of tension there."

All these adverbs and modifiers were driving her crazy. What did it say about you as a person that another's heartfelt confession brought on the urge to edit? Why were people so messy with language? Didn't anyone think before they spoke?

Yet again Thorn pulled at his thumb and ran a finger down his wrist. The cuff slid back and Cerridwen caught her breath. There was a scar, faint and badly healed, puckering the skin of his inner arm. A flood of questions rose. It fell again before she opened her mouth. She was not going to be stupid this time. She would not act like a heroine from a penny dreadful.

What she needed to do was stem the flow or get Jane in here. As interesting as this all was in reality, Jane was the one qualified to deal with this surreal situation. Cerridwen told Thorn that she'd just remembered something and then went out into the hall without waiting for a reply.

Fred glanced up with a frown as she left. That might have been because the Aga was winning. Carl, with her back door in pieces on the floor around him, didn't even notice.

Thomas and Gerry had just come in with a bunch of groceries. Now this wasn't so bad. Maybe she could talk one of them into doing her laundry before this was over.

"Anyone seen Jane recently?" she queried the room at large.

"She's gone up the block to talk to a man about some graffiti," Gerry offered.

"Thorn is in my kitchen pouring his heart out. Somebody take him a glass of water, or something stronger, while I go find Jane." She got out on to the front steps and grabbed the railing to steady herself while she took deep breaths. She would go and get Jane. Jane would deal with it.

Thomas came out of the house. "What's going on? You're freaking out."

"Thorn broke into my house."

"What, right now? I thought Fred let him in." Thomas turned back towards the house.

"No, He's the intruder from last night." He was right. She really wanted to freak out.

"You didn't see the intruder." Thomas tensed. She resolved to never tell him he looked like a wolf on the hunt.

"I saw his hand when I hit him with the door. He has a scar running from the base of his thumb, down his wrist. It healed badly and it's kind of distinctive."

"I'll kill him! No, I'll get Jane and she'll kill him." Thomas took off.

She had to run to keep up. "I think I can make it to the end of the street in relative safety," Cerridwen said.

"And I'm sure that Joan thought she was perfectly safe in her own bedroom. And Ms. Hawkner probably thought she was in no danger in her own front yard. And you thought you were safe last night when that nut job broke into your house. None of us goes anywhere alone. Besides, I need to borrow Jane's gun." Thomas was being his most reasonable and patient. He probably used that tone with badly behaved first graders. She might find time later to resent that.

"I'm sure you would be fine until I got back." She couldn't resist needling him. It didn't work. She should have known better than to try and get a rise out of someone who worked with children on a daily basis. He just shrugged.

"Think of it as a sop to my male ego. If I'm busy making sure you're never alone, then I'm never alone. Safety in numbers without wounding my male psyche. Or you could go, and I could go back to the house and bash Thorn's skull in." He punctuated the last statement by batting his ridiculously long eyelashes at her.

"He's more than twice your age. You'd get jail time. Or he might win, and that would just be embarrassing." Cerridwen tucked her arm through his. Not an easy thing to do with the height difference. "I love you. At times I want to kill you, but I do love you."

"Yeah, but from you that's a sign of affection," Thomas pointed out.

They came to the open space in front of Whitmore's grand gate. The red letters were even more garish in light of day. The pain it would cause Joan gave the ugliness an extra kick. To deface the home that meant so much to her would have been a low blow at any time. But added to the events of the last few weeks it was like kicking a puppy. It was hurtful. And Cerridwen was damned if she could see what purpose it served.

Jane was trying to talk to Mr. Demetriov with little success. He admitted to no English though Cerridwen suspected he understood more than he let on. And there were no grandchildren to interpret the strange mix of Russian and Spanish that he and his wife had developed over the past decades. He simply stood by his pressure washer and smiled and nodded at her attempts at communication.

"You don't understand a word I'm saying, do you?" Jane said brightly. Mr. Demetriov gave her an encouraging nod.

"And you don't care either," she added. "Just nod and smile if you have no idea what I'm talking about."

Mr. Demetriov nodded and smiled.

"Great, just great." Jane rubbed her temples.

"Problem?" Cerridwen asked.

"He has been trying to tell me something for the last thirty minutes. But there is a bit of a language barrier and I've never been very good at charades."

"Doesn't the police department have interpreters?" Thomas asked.

"Yes. But none of them speak Russian. And his grandchildren have either gone to school or stolen a bus and driven into the ocean. Some of his gestures were a little ambiguous." Jane shrugged.

Thomas turned to Mr. Demetriov and spoke in rapid fire Russian. Both women turned to stare at him. Mr. Demetriov lit up like a Christmas tree.

Exchanges translated by his grandchildren were usually brief and to the point. While he was working, he never talked much, opening his mouth only when he felt it was necessary. The flood of words was unprecedented.

"Can you understand him?" Jane demanded.

"Fairly well," Thomas allowed. "It's a slightly different dialect than I'm used to. And the occasional Spanish word is throwing me off a bit. But I think I've got the gist."

"What is he saying?" Jane showed rare impatience.

"This is not the same as it was the first time," Thomas told her. He paused to listen. "In the 60s, when it happened the first time, there were two." He frowned. "Two what?" he muttered under his breath. "Oh I see. There were two people painting the graffiti like this. You could tell from the way the letters were formed. Does he mean handwriting? One, clearly a copycat, showed here and there down in the town proper. I think that's what he means."

The words were coming thick and fast now. Mr. Demetriov's hands had turned into birds fluttering here and there as if, at any moment, he would break into an interpretive dance. Thomas's eyebrows shot up nearly to his hairline. He broke in to ask something.

Mr. Demetriov, ecstatic at being understood, nodded firmly and repeated his statement slower, emphasizing each word. He then pointed at Jane, encouraging Thomas to pass on what he had said.

"The other person, the one he thinks started it, was Joan."

Both women made startled noises, but Thomas wasn't looking at them. He maintained eye contact with Mr. Demetriov who continued to make "go on" gestures at him. "He knows it was her because he caught her at it once. He thinks she did it more than once because he saw other examples where the letters looked the same. Mr. Witt was very upset." Thomas stopped speaking as Mr. Demetriov fired another volley of Russian.

"Mr. Witt didn't want anyone to know. He had him clean off the paint before anyone else could see it. Although a couple of times he thinks he might not have been fast enough. Witt took Joan to a doctor. A head doctor, he says. Does he mean psychiatrist? Witt was very worried. He said not to tell anyone anything about anything."

The older man stepped closer to Thomas and jabbed at him with his finger.

"Mr. Witt thought that Joan killed Mary. But Mr. Demetriov does not think that. He does not think this is possible. It is more possible that someone wanted him, Mr. Witt, to think this. Maybe it suits this person that Witt thinks this. He does not know. He does know that this time it is not Joan. The letters are wrong. That is all he has to say about it. And now he is going to go back to work."

Mr. Demetriov drove his point home by turning on the pressure washer. They had to move back to avoid getting sprayed.

A movement near the gate caught Cerridwen's eye. Stone stood on the steps of Whitmore watching the cleanup operation. Had he heard what they had said? He wore an expression she could not quite translate. It might have been irritation. But at what? It was oddly familiar. For a second, it was almost as if she was seeing him in black and white. He stood there and watched Mr. Demetriov. And then the moment was gone as he turned and wandered down the drive towards them.

"I knew you could swear in Russian, but I didn't realize you were fluent," Cerridwen said to Thomas.

"It's not uncommon for children and grandchildren of immigrants to have limited fluency in their antecedents' language," Stone offered as he approached. "Can you understand the gardener? I can't get anything out of him."

"Do you speak Russian?" Thomas asked.

"No," Stone confessed.

"Well, there's your problem right there." Thomas shrugged.

"How well do you speak it?"

"Well enough to get by in most, but not all situations." Thomas grinned at him. "There are topics I don't have the vocabulary to cover."

"What topics?" Cerridwen was curious.

Sheepish looked strange on some of Thomas' size. "I had a girlfriend in college who wanted me to talk dirty to her in Russian."

"Maybe I don't want to hear this," Cerridwen said.

"Yeah, but I do," Stone said.

"Well, Dedushka and Dyadya did not use those kinds of words in front of me. I was at a loss for a bit."

"Dedushka and Dyadya?" Jane stepped off the sidewalk where an encroaching bush had spread.

"Grandpa and uncle," Thomas clarified, holding a low branch out of the way. "So I improvised. It worked for a while, till she recognized the word for beet and figured out that I was reciting a recipe for borscht. She dumped me not long after. It was all very awkward."

Chapter 23

As they headed back to her house, Cerridwen could only reflect on how irritating real life was. The problem was, she decided not for the first time, that it was badly plotted. Loose threads everywhere, and no thought to continuity. Mess is what real life was, although there was all kinds of character development going on around her.

Between Mr. Demetriov's revelation and Thomas' confession, Cerridwen almost forgot to tell Jane about Thorn, still sitting in her kitchen. Cerridwen summarized while Thomas growled under his breath. And somehow, when they had gone back to the house, Stone had come with them. Cerridwen longed for the days when her house was quiet and she hardly ever had unwanted guests or break-ins.

In her absence, Fred had chosen to give Thorn vodka instead of water, the end result being he was no use to anyone, Jane was mad, and there were still people cluttering up Cerridwen's kitchen. In the middle of this, Stone handed her the phone and told her that Topless Lilith wanted to talk to her. She was entirely at a loss until she heard Mrs. Gray's voice at the other end. Everyone wanted something today. Cerridwen took a deep breath, reminded herself patience was a virtue, that none of them meant to be a bother, and silently vowed to kill them all horrifically in the next book.

"What can I do for you, Mrs. Gray?" It occurred to her that, barring Teddy's revelation last night, she had never heard the woman referenced as anything else. How did you go from "Topless Lilith" to an impenetrable armor of respectability? If she could figure that out, she could use it for a character. Cerridwen started to build the person in her mind but was brought back to reality sharply by Mrs. Gray's voice.

"Did you leave a message for me, dear? With the Historical Society?"

"Not for you specifically. It was about my locks. I am having them replaced in an effort to prevent everybody and his brother from waltzing through my front door. Someone in your organization took it upon themselves to suggest that Carl the locksmith was sexually assaulting my house. I was calling to reassure you that all the necessary attention was being paid to historical detail. And that I take my home's preservation very seriously." She winced to hear herself use the word very. If she wanted information out of Mrs. Gray, she needed to stay on her good side.

"Oh, I see." Cerrridwen felt a little guilty as a thread of exhaustion wove through Mrs. Gray's voice. "I had hoped it was about the furniture exhibit. Your great grandmother had a mechanical table that would perfectly fill a little gap we have. I understand she purchased it from Mr. Witt, and we've been at some bother to track it down." The touch of reproach in Mrs. Gray's voice, as if Cerridwen should have known she had the table and volunteered it immediately the Historical Society decided they wanted it, helped her guilt recede just a bit. Cerridwen wasn't even sure which of the hundred plus tables in her house the Society in the person of Mrs. Gray was talking about.

"We would, of course, love to borrow it for our exhibition. But that was not my primary reason for calling." Mrs. Gray's armor was back on.

Cerridwen toyed with the idea of loaning the table for the karma points, if only she had any clue which one it was. Maybe she could just throw them any table.

"The real reason I called was to solicit your aid on another matter. Joan and Jason are determined to go ahead with their Halloween party this weekend. Jason feels it would give his mother something positive to focus on. And the invitations have already gone out. The problem is, neither of them has done the slightest bit to get ready for it."

"Well, to be fair, they've both had other things on their minds," Cerridwen pointed out gently.

"I am aware of that, of course." There was a note of irritation in Mrs. Gray's voice. "But it still leaves a lot to be done. I simply wanted to let you know that everything is on track for Saturday. I wouldn't turn down help if you had a few minutes here and there."

First Cerridwen's furniture, and now free labor? The woman didn't want much, did she? But it was more for Joan than her. And was it really fair to dislike Mrs. Gray for being perfect?

"I will see what I can do. The next few days are very busy for me. I am behind schedule as it is." Cerridwen could hear her own voice becoming more clipped, her sentences getting shorter. The men in her kitchen had all turned to look at her with different degrees of curiosity on their faces. She really couldn't find the strength to care at this point. The world was one long distraction today, and she was done with it.

Jane emerged from the office with a worse-for-wear Thorn in tow. She wanted to know who had given him the vodka and how he had gotten into the house in the first place. As voices tripped over themselves in explanations, Cerridwen snuck into her office and closed and locked the door.

A whole day down the drain and she hadn't gotten any work done. Apparently her schedule was just going to be shot to hell until this was over. Whatever this was. All sorts of information had been dumped in her lap, but it was all so disorganized. She had no idea what to do with any of it. Yet another way books were different from reality. In fiction you could just beat it into shape till it made sense. In real life, shit just happened, and it was really annoying.

Joan had been responsible for the first round of graffiti. Her father had taken this as a sign that she was responsible for whatever had happened to Mary. But was that what it meant? Or was a frightened child searching for answers to something she didn't understand in the only way she knew how? Joan couldn't have been more than eleven or twelve at the time. Was that the only reason he had for thinking Joan had done it? Cerridwen was more inclined to believe that Joan had seen something deeply traumatizing. It certainly fit her behavior now.

When Mary had disappeared without a trace, Thorn had locked up her room to keep it safe and there it had stayed for decades. Had they expected her to come back for her things someday, or did no one care? Thorn claimed he had a thing for her and yet he seemed to do as little as anyone else when she disappeared. So he had left at the end of the summer. Did it never occur to him to find out if she came back?

None of it made any sense. So many damn questions Cerridwen didn't have the answers to. She was starting to sound like one of those trade paperbacks where they padded their word count with a summing up every twenty five pages or so. Screw it all—she would worry about everything tomorrow.

Chapter 24

Cerridwen listened to the sounds of the old house settling around her. The sounds mixed with the sounds of the mattress settling under Thomas. If she intended to keep him, she would have to acquire a larger mattress at some point, and by default a larger bed frame. She was rather fond of the gilt swirls, but Thomas was long enough to bump his head and his feet at the same time.

Did she want to keep him? Did she want to be the older woman? It was only a few years, but it was always less acceptable when the woman was the older one. "The older writer with the younger, hot bass player. Look at me, Mom, I'm Jackie Collins," she mumbled.

Thomas didn't seem to mind. His steady breathing told her he had found the sleep that eluded her.

It probably wouldn't have bothered her grandmother, either. Three of her husbands had been younger than her. Cerridwen had no idea how much younger. Constance Frey's exact age had been a carefully guarded secret.

Something pulled at the edge of her mind. Something about secrets. She had heard or seen something recently, something about tables.

"Mechanical!" Cerridwen dislodged Thomas, clipping his jaw with the top of her head as she sat up. He rolled to the side and hit his shoulder on the night stand.

"What?" He rubbed his chin.

"She said mechanical."

"I know, I heard her." There was a note of sarcasm in his voice. "And I don't find it at all creepy that she's talking about herself in the third person."

"No, not me! Mrs. Gray. Before she said marquetry, or antique. But earlier, on the phone she said mechanical." She scrambled across him, out of the bed and went to the dressing table. He sighed as drawers opened and slammed.

"Seriously?" he inquired of the gold leafed plaster ceiling before moving. He hauled himself out of the bed, a process that involved a lot of unfolding.

She opened and closed drawers in the mirrored dressing table till she found a tiny gold key.

"There are way too many keys around this place," Thomas said before Ceridwen pushed past him and all but skipped down the stairs and along the hall. In the little room at the back of the house, she shoved the couch to one side to better get at the end table. Because it wasn't really an end table.

"Would you like some help?" His voice dripped with patience.

"I need this table out where I can get at it. It's stuffed between the couch and the wall so it won't open." She stretched and tugged, to no purpose.

With another sigh he lifted the table up and over the arm of the couch and set it on the floor in front of her. He gazed at the ceiling and blew a stray hair out of his eyes as she felt around the edge of the table, muttering under her breath. She let out a crow of triumph when she found what she was looking for.

"What are you doing?" Jane inquired from the doorway where she stood in her pajamas, gun drawn. "I thought someone had broken in again. Nice pajama bottoms, by the way."

"I like Eeyore. He has a practical streak that appeals to me on a very deep level," Thomas responded with dignity.

"Mechanical furniture often served the same purpose as a modern safe," Cerridwen said, crouching on the floor and ignoring this byplay. "Hiding valuables in secret compartments that were all but invisible from the outside, undetectable unless you knew where to look. And now I know where to look. Grandma's journal said where a lady hides her secrets. I didn't think till just now that she meant that in a more literal sense." Cerridwen ran her fingers across the wood. Jane pulled gloves out of the pocket of her pajamas. Jane was never unprepared.

A lady in full court dress danced across the inlaid wood top with a unicorn in attendance. When you put the key in the lock on the front, the top slid back, and another panel slid forward to form a writing desk. A quick search of the three drawers and a tiny sliding compartment revealed very little.

"Letters, some postcards. A couple of photos. Oh, my." Jane's widened her eyes. She held the objects out of reach as Thomas tried to peer over her head.

"But nothing that would tell us who killed Mary." Cerridwen plopped on the rug with a groan.

"Don't give up hope yet." Jane lifted something small and shiny from inside one of the little drawers.

"Oh great, another key." Thomas flopped on the couch. It was too low to be comfortable and he looked at them from between his knees. "What does that one go to? How many locks does one house need?"

"We would only need one." Jane ran her gloved hands over the wood, examining the table from every angle.

"What are you looking for? A secret compartment in the secret compartment?" asked Thomas.

Neither woman was listening.

"Try this end. There seems to be more table than drawer." Cerridwen pointed. Jane slid to the other end.

"And even if there is yet another secret compartment, just what is going to be in it anyway? A signed confession and a photo of the murder posing in front of the tree?" No sooner were the words out of his mouth than there was a click. Jane sat on the rug, tiny key in hand, peering into the now visible drawer. Cerridwen scrambled off the floor.

"Are you kidding me!" Thomas surged to his feet.

"It's not a signed confession. It's an account book," Jane lifted a leather bound ledger out of the drawer. "More specifically, Witt's account book."

"Is that one of the books Thorn had the day Mary disappeared? It might be what they argued over." Cerridwen tried to work out where this new information fit.

"Either way, I think we may have found a reason for someone to kill Mary Paul."

Chapter 25

The inhabitants of Witt's End were forced to follow their late night with an early morning. Jane, of course, had evidence to process, an investigation to run, and a forensic accountant to lay hands on. The others would have stayed in bed but for the doorbell.

The first ear-splitting peal ushered in Ruby, dragging a frazzled Mrs. Gray behind her. Mrs. Gray was probably regretting her pleas for help. Ruby had answered with a vengeance. It seemed in all the excitement the Witt's had forgotten to book any musicians for the party they were still determined to hold on Saturday. And, of course, it was impossible to get anyone at so late a date.

"But you're a musician, dear," Ruby beamed at Thomas. "You and your friends. Gerry keeps talking about your band, and I thought I'd solve more than one problem with one stone." Ruby mixed metaphors without compunction. "And I told Lilith here that I'm sure you boys wouldn't mind helping out. Course, I'm sure Joan will pay you. Once she has her head on again, obviously."

Amusement and doubt battled each other for Thomas's expression. "What kind of music did you have in mind?" His tone was cautious.

"I wouldn't venture an opinion," Mrs. Gray said. It was clear she felt her opinion would make no difference to hurricane Ruby.

"Oh, whatever you think is best, dear. Of course, you will take it being Halloween into account. And it is a party, after all. So make your choices accordingly. As long as it doesn't involve an actual accordion."

"Well, that certainly narrows it down a bit." Thomas was trying very hard not to laugh.

"I know you'll come up with something. There is a piano on site that you can use. There are probably other instruments lying about you could use as well. And I assume you have some of your own. Bring whatever you feel you need with you. And I'll talk to Joan about time and payment and all that." Everything settled to her satisfaction, Ruby swept out again, drawing along a thoroughly out-maneuvered Mrs. Gray in her wake.

Cerridwen sighed. Ruby swept off so fast there had been no chance to pick Mrs. Gray's brain about the past or her interest in a certain table.

Once they left, Thomas laid his head down on the kitchen table and laughed till tears streamed down his face. Cerridwen was worried that he was going to hurt himself on the marble. But he sat up unharmed, though still struggling for breath. "Mrs. Gray is going to be sorry she didn't venture an opinion. Or at least ask what we play."

"Why's that?" Cerridwen handed him a napkin to wipe his streaming eyes.

"We all play a variety of music. But what we play most, what we play together… what we play really well is metal." He shook with anticipated mirth. "Oh, to see her face Saturday when she realizes she's booked a metal band."

"You don't think Ruby will care?" Cerridwen decided this was a dumb question as soon as she asked it. Thomas was thinking along the same lines.

"Nah. Ruby knows. It's probably half the reason she did it," he answered absently. He was already running over a set list in his head. "It will have to be mostly covers. Not ideal, but with only two days to plan it, better to stick with stuff we already knew cold." Before he could further contemplate Ruby's reaction to metal music—much less Mrs. Gray's reaction—the door bell screamed again. Cerridwen started to get up. Thomas waved her back into her seat and went to answer the door. He returned to the kitchen a short time later with Joan and Jason in tow.

The Witts had switched roles this morning. Cerridwen wondered if it would be permanent. Jason held his mother's hand as he led her into the room. She held back like a reluctant child. The competent, confident Joan of last week was nowhere to be found. It was heartbreaking.

"If it's about Saturday, Ruby and Mrs. Gray have already been," she told them as she began to clear the table.

"My mother has something she would like to say to you, Cerridwen." Jason nudged Joan into a chair.

Joan sulked for a moment and then took a deep breath. "Cerridwen, I am sorry I broke into your house and hit you over the head. I thought you were an intruder. I mean, another intruder besides me."

"I understand, honey. You explained the other day. But why did you need to break into my house, Joan? What were you looking for?"

"My father kept a journal. I was going to give them to Stone to use for the book. But I meant to pull the one that covered Mary's disappearance." Joan took a shaky breath, close to tears. "I know my father thought I had something to do with it. I never convinced him otherwise. I wanted to hide that one. I didn't want people to know that he thought that. But it was already gone."

"But why would you think it would be here?" Cerridwen had assumed the journal Joan referred to the other day had been her grandmother's. She could not think of a reason that Constance would have Witt's journal. They had not been close. From what she could remember, getting Mary that job had been their closest interaction. Grandma had little tolerance for stupidity and had held Witt in mild contempt.

"I couldn't find it in the house. I looked everywhere. I knew Constance had collected what she thought was evidence. She could have had it. She could have thought that I did it. She asked me so many questions." Joan was shaking again. "I didn't, you know. I would never have hurt Mary."

"Constance didn't think you had done it. She thought you might have seen what happened, but she never thought it was you." Cerridwen's heart ached for the young, frightened Joan. How utterly the adults in her life had failed her, got knowing what had happened to her friend and living in fear of punishment for a crime Cerridwen was now convinced Joan had not committed. "He never gave her the journal. He wouldn't even talk to her about Mary."

"He sold her the table," Joan whispered.

The word table brought the kitchen to a standstill. Cerridwen looked to Jane. Jane made keep going motions with her hands.

"What table?"

"The mechanical table that used to sit in the estate office. Daddy sold it to Constance. There was a book in there. I thought it was his journal."

"So you knew there was something in there when your father sold the table. Is it possible he didn't know?" Jane asked.

Joan thought about this. "It never occurred to me he didn't. But I never did see him open it."

"Is that what the other person was looking for?" Cerridwen asked, sparing a thought for the little lacquered table she hadn't found the time to glue back together.

"It's possible someone knew about the table. But not what it looked like," said Joan. "You'll have to tell the Historical Society that they have to borrow another table. That isn't everything." She took a shaky breath. "The key. You asked about, I had it."

Cerridwen felt cold all over as her attention was grabbed by the use of the past tense.

"Had?"

"I lost it." Joan had shrunk in on herself. "I had it the night that I..." She couldn't bring herself to say she had hit Cerridwen. So she skated clumsily past it. "I lost it. I think the other person may have it."

Cerridwen struggled with evaporating sympathy. She had suspected that Joan had lost the key. Confirming that Joan had done just that, and not considered the danger it put Cerridwen in, was still unsettling.

"I'm sorry. I didn't know what to do." Joan was a frightened and defensive child again.

Cerridwen had made excuses for Joan all along, but now she wondered how much of Joan's behavior was because of trauma and how much was sheer self-centeredness. At no point had she considered that she was endangering other people. It was getting harder to ignore that.

"Who has the key, Joan?"

"I don't know!"

"Who was in my house, Joan?" Cerridwen's voice rose.

"I told you I don't know!" Joan was getting angry now.

"Get out." Cerridwen didn't raise her voice this time. She was just too tired. *Let Jane dig for the truth in Joan's story.*

"I was trying to apologize." Joan started to cry. "I didn't think about what it meant. I should have, I should have thought what it meant when I got home and couldn't find the key. But I was scared. It was bringing it all back. It was like it was happening all over again. Do you understand? I didn't mean it. I just didn't think."

"Just go."

Joan got up and followed her son to the door. She stopped just outside the kitchen as if the threshold was a barrier against Cerridwen's pain. She made a visible effort to pull herself together.

"I didn't kill Mary, I don't know who did. And I'm sorry I broke into your house and hit you over the head. That is all I wanted to say." They were the words of a grownup, delivered in the defiant voice of a child who knew she was in trouble. Once again, there were two Joans.

"She knew there was another key," Cerridwen said to Thomas. "For three weeks she knew that someone was out there with a way into my house and she didn't tell me."Cerridwen wondered if she was expecting too much of someone in a weakened mental state. Maybe, but the sense of betrayal was hard to shake.

Cerridwen shut herself in her office and vented her spleen by brutally murdering two minor characters. She then spent a frustrating two hours trying to fit their bloody end into the plot. She could hear Thomas moving about in the kitchen. Sometime later, Jane's voice penetrated the office door. It was nearly one when Thomas waved the white flag of lunch through a narrow opening between door and jam.

Jane sat at the kitchen table drawing a pattern on the marble with her finger. She looked tired, but it was overshadowed by what Cerridwen thought of as Jane's thinking face.

"Someone was skimming from Witt's business accounts as well as the income from the Witt Estate. What little income the estate was bringing in. Together, it was no small amount and easy to find if you know what you're looking for. And Mary Paul knew what she was looking for. According to the forensic accountant, he didn't have to do any real work, just follow her notes. The thing is annotated within an inch of its life. The only problem being that there are no account numbers or anything of that nature. Most of the withdrawals were made in cash. The rest is hidden in household or business expenses."

"So who kept the books before Mary showed up to kill the goose that laid the golden egg?" Thomas dumped a handful of silverware on the table.

"Our forensic accountant is working on that. Evidently a number of people made entries in the book over the years. Then all the 'disciples' scattered when Witt died. Nobody that I've been able to reach is quite sure who was supposed to be running the various Witt business interests for that period."

"So, if she had the ledger, why didn't Constance go to the police?" Thomas asked.

"With what?" Cerridwen was resigned.

"She had proof that someone was robbing Witt blind," he pointed out.

"Yeah, but she didn't know who. And she had no proof that it was connected to Mary's disappearance. And she was the only one that said that Mary had disappeared at all," Cerridwen told him.

Jane nodded in glum agreement. You knew it was bad when normally poised Jane did glum.

"So, they all just though their friend had wandered off and would come back when she felt like it? Or did they think she had just ascended into the ether?" Thomas wanted to know.

"The ones that noticed, or cared that she was gone. Thorn thought she was avoiding him," Cerridwen pointed out.

"Joan thought Mary left because she was ill. And Joan's father assumed that Joan had killed Mary."

"But why? Why would you assume you're your eleven year old had murdered someone?" Thomas dished out pasta. "It seems a damn stupid conclusion to leap to."

Jane looked at him with eyes narrowed.

Cerridwen was the one to say out loud what she and Jane were both thinking.

"Because someone wanted him to believe it. Someone told Witt that Mary was dead and that Joan had done it. And convincingly enough that he believed them."

"The only reason I could think to do that would be to cover the fact that you had done it yourself," Jane said.

"So are Mary's predecessor and the murderer one and the same?'

"It makes the most sense," Jane agreed.

Thomas was silent as he watched the two women toss ideas to each other like a tennis match.

"Joan doesn't know who it is. That's why she needs to find her father's journal," Jane added.

"But someone thinks she does. That's why 'someone' tried to kill her with the sleeping pills," Cerridwen said with certainty.

"If it was a murder attempt, it had to be someone in the house that night. We know of Jason, Stone, Mrs. Gray, and the nurse that was supposed to be monitoring her when Joan overdosed. Was there someone in the house...and if so, who?"

"Hard to believe in a lurking stranger—and I don't see any reason for the nurse to do it," Cerridwen said dismissively.

"If this was a book it would be one or the other," Jane said.

"Yeah, but you keep telling me it's not. So we strike the stranger and the nurse. Next is Jason."

"He's too young," Thomas interjected.

"To kill Mary. But there is the house," Cerridwen offered.

"You think he would kill his mother over the house?" Thomas was horrified.

"To save the house, maybe. He loves that crumbling pile. But you're right, he couldn't have killed Mary, and we agreed it was the same person." Cerridwen sighed.

"We could be wrong," Jane pointed out.

"Well, there is always a chance of that. But we will skip Jason for now. So it's between Stone and Mrs. Gray." Cerridwen ticked off her fingers. "Stone makes a good lurking stranger, too."

"Don't forget Thorn," Thomas said.

Both women contemplated this for a moment.

"Thomas's right. Thorn has as much reason as anyone else. He was in the neighborhood and that house is not exactly Fort Knox." Cerridwen gave it serious thought.

"So we have talked ourselves right back to square one." Jane drummed her fingers in frustration.

"Square one is getting damn familiar." Cerridwen threw her hands up as Jane's phone rang. Jane went out into the hall to answer it. They could hear her pacing the floor, from the door, to the stairs, to the occasional table, and back.

Cerridwen ate her pasta with a viciousness that did little to relieve her frustration.

"You know, I never get tired of that," Thomas said from across the table. The chair registered a token protest as he dropped into it but held firm. She was going to have to get sturdier furniture.

"Never get tired of what?" Cerridwen asked around a mouthful of noodles.

"The happy, slightly crazed look you get in your eye when you think about murder. It's kind of sexy."

She wondered what that statement said about their relationship. A psychologist would probably have a field day with both of them.

Chapter 26

Cerridwen bowed to the inevitable. She could ignore the whooshing sound of approaching deadlines for one day. There was no way anyone living in Green Man Court was getting out of helping with the party. Not even Felix had managed to escape Ruby's web of guilt and bribes, something he was normally quite good at. The two of them were in the grand entrance hall wrapping lights around the banister and up across the gallery.

"I'm still not sure what happened," he grumbled as he held the ladder for Cerridwen. "One moment I'm orchestrating Hadrian's seduction by a Celtic princess, and the next I'm stringing fairy lights."

"Did Hadrian ever go to Britain?" Cerridwen teetered at the top of the ladder as she stretched, trying to reach a particularly high Gothic squiggle on the woodwork. She settled for tossing the string of lights until they snagged.

"Why does everyone ask that? Whatever happened to willing suspension of disbelieve?" The ladder wobbled as Felix threw his arms in the air.

"I think you killed it when the Empress Theodosia overthrew her husband and lead the Byzantines to victory against the Goths."

"You think there's a plot hole?"

"Not so much a plot hole as a gaping chasm in the timeline."

"Hmm. Maybe we could work it out with some roleplay. Want to help me act it out?" Felix wiggled his eyebrows.

"Nice try, but you are not getting out of this with a clumsy come-on. I've been onto that one since college." She tossed another loop of lights. It missed and fell across her shoulder, dangling down her back.

"You don't believe you're my everything? Cerridwen, I'm hurt. Wounded even." Felix clutched his chest and staggered a bit for effect.

"Honey, I don't even believe I'm your only. You're just a little indiscriminate." She started down the ladder. "And we need more extension cord."

"Everyone's a critic. First my work and now my love life," Felix complained. "I do discriminate, just not on the basis of gender." He went off to look for the cord, still mumbling under his breath and waving his arms. He passed Stone, who gave him a wide berth on his way to the bottom of the ladder.

Stone righted the ladder as it wobbled. "Need some help there?" he asked.

"No thanks. I'm at a standstill till I have another extension cord." Cerridwen would have stepped down, but Stone didn't move. His face was a blank—a careful, deliberate, blank. His knuckles turned white as he gripped the ladder.

"The floor is uneven," he told her. She hadn't noticed any unevenness. The floor had been placidly level all morning. She was only three steps up, but that still put her a good four feet up. If she fell from here, she might get a few bumps or bruises. Or she might crack her head open on the hardwood floor. This was the point in the story where the heroine would feel a shiver of fear.

"How did you know?" Stone asked. He seemed genuinely curious. Too bad she had no idea what he was talking about.

"Excuse me?" She took another step down, but he didn't move.

"Did your roommate tell you?" He persisted.

"Jane? Jane tells me lots of things. There are also a lot of things she doesn't tell me. Blabbing is not encouraged in her line of work."

"You're telling me you really don't know?" His tone was thick with disbelieve.

"If you told me what we were talking about, I might be better able to answer you." Unease and irritation struggled for the upper hand. If he tipped the ladder now, she was still high enough to be badly hurt. But he wouldn't get to the point.

"You really don't. It was just a shot in the dark. Shit!" Stone laughed and banged a fist against the rung below her. Cerridwen clung as the step ladder shook. The unease was winning. Where was Felix? How long did it take to find an extension cord, for Christ sake?

"I can't answer that since I still have no idea what you are talking about." It probably wasn't a good idea to antagonize him. But as long as he was talking, he wasn't tipping her onto the floor.

He released his grip, stepping away from her. Cerridwen stifled a sigh of relief. "The other night at the hospital. You said that doctor was probably Mary Paul's long-lost-something." He watched her scramble to the floor with calm detachment.

"I have a dim memory of it. I probably said a lot of things. I hadn't had a lot of sleep. And quite a bit of trauma. It's been going around." On closer inspection, the floor still seemed perfectly even.

Cerridwen hurriedly backed against the wall as he came closer. Maybe she would have been safer on the ladder. Seriously, where had Felix gone for that extension cord, outer Mongolia?

"You weren't taunting me?" Couldn't the man pick between scary and baffling, even he was losing track of the conversation? Was she imagining the menace? His tone was so casual.

"Why would I taunt you?" Fear gave way to exasperation.

"Mary Paul was my aunt."

"Should I say congratulations, or I'm sorry?" This news explained a few inconsistencies. For instance, Stone's habit of leading any conversation about the Witt firmly in the direction of Mary at the slightest opportunity. His reaction to her comments in the ER came back to her in Technicolor. He studied her closely and then moved away. Cerridwen took a deep breath.

"She was my mother's older sister. I never knew her, but Mom worshiped her. She still does. And she doesn't know what happened to her. One day she was just gone, poof!" He threw his hands in the air. "Because someone stuffed her in a tree." His voice rose sharply. Cerridwen pressed harder against the wall. He took another step, bringing his face close to hers. She could hear footsteps at last.

"So, I came to find out what happened to her. Then people start dying, which believe me was not part of the plan. And out of the blue you just happen to say, hey, maybe Mary's long lost something has come for revenge."

"I was guessing, thinking out loud. It made a good story." Cerridwen shrugged. "You're a writer. You understand a good story." She could hear Felix in the hall.

Stone laughed. Some of the tension left him, he shook his head. "Yeah, I get it. But you threw me for a loop. I thought you were messing with me." He gave the ladder a nudge. "So you got this? I told Ruby I would help with the flowers."

Jane and Felix appeared in the doorway behind him.

"Yeah, thanks. There's Felix with my cord." She would have to ask just how far he had to go to find it. Stone nodded to the newcomers as he moved around them.

Felix turned to watch him go. "What's that about?"

"Mary Paul had a sister," Cerridwen told him.

"Susan Paul married a professor at Berkeley. His last name was Stone. Their only child Michael Stone is Mary Paul's 'long lost' nephew," Jane said.

"Didn't I say?" Cerridwen crowed.

"You said Blue Scrubs was her long-lost-something," Felix pointed out.

"Details. So I was off slightly. No one gets it right the first draft. And it made him swallow his tongue, remember. I should have picked up on that."

"Yes, but it makes everything else go pear shaped." Jane sighed.

"How long have you known?" Cerridwen asked.

"Since yesterday. How long have you known?" Jane countered.

Cerridwen made a show of looking at the clock. "Oh, less than half an hour. Just since Stone cornered me on the ladder and made me very nervous. He assumed I already knew because of what I said in the hospital the other night. He thought I was baiting him."

"Do you think Stone killed Hawkner out of revenge?" Felix dumped a pile of extension cords on the floor.

"Motive is the last thing the police look at," Jane reminded them. "Have I taught you people nothing?"

"Did he have the opportunity to kill Hawkner?"

"Everybody had opportunity to kill Hawkner. And he certainly had opportunity to give Joan the sleeping pills. And we did not have this conversation." Jane remembered who she was talking to. "I have some paperwork to finish. I'll see you guys tonight." She left with a wave.

"So what was she doing here, I wonder?" Cerridwen asked Felix.

He shrugged. "I don't know. She was talking to Joan about something. I have brought you every extension cord in the house." He threw the massive coil he had been holding at her feet. They both contemplated it for a moment.

"Somebody is going to come looking for those."

"Yes," he agreed.

"We should probably use as many as we can before that happens."

With almost identical sighs of resignation, they went back to work.

Chapter 27

Cerridwen got ready for Joan's party in a state of abstraction. Mary Paul was very much in her mind as she pinned her wild curls up and under in a faux bob, for all the good it did her. She thought herself in circles and was no closer to answer as she wiggled into one of her great grandmother's evening gowns from the 1920s. It was backless and cut nearly to her belly button, the deep blue silk gathered and held in place by strategic bands of silver that matched her jeweled headband. If she accomplished nothing else tonight, she was damn well going to make a splash.

She and Teddy walked up the street to Whitmore. Her four inch T strap heels made the garden path an impossibility. Teddy had chosen to dress as a Roman gladiator, so his footwear was nearly as impractical. The gravel drive was an obstacle course of service vehicles. Between them, Ruby and Mrs. Gray had beaten the local caters into submission. Even with the late start the party seemed to be coming off with little difficulty. The house was a blaze of lights.

Cerridwen had not seen Thomas or his house mates all day as they ferried their equipment up to Whitmore. Ruby had flitted here and there in a cloud of chiffon and bossiness. Cerridwen had yet to lay eyes on Mrs. Gray. That was not by accident. She had no intention of being pressed into more labor or nagged about furniture. And chances to question Mrs. Gray or Joan would be thin on the ground if she could even figure out what to ask them.

Ruby and Mrs. Gray were arguing in the entrance hall over the enormous oleander that had stood in the sun room on Cerridwen's last visit. It was now smack in front of the front doors. Mrs. Gray was determined to move it. Ruby was just as adamant that it was staying.

"Joan wants it here. And we mustn't lose sight of the fact it is Joan's party." Ruby was using the condescending tone she used on people she felt needed to have proper behavior explained to them. Any minute she would call Mrs. Gray "Dear." Mrs. Gray, predictably, would not be put in her place.

"It is in the way. You can barely get around it. Surely we could push it back a bit." None of that was phrased as a question. The reminder that it was Joan's party irked Mrs. Gray. Because she had done most of the work, wondered Cerridwen. Or it bothered her to be placed subordinate to someone she still perceived as a child. She turned to the newcomers for support. Teddy pretended deep interest in the ceiling. Cerridwen was saved from having to answer by the arrival of their hostess.

"It could go a little closer to the stairs, if necessary," Joan said as she swept down the stairs in question in full Victorian regalia. Cerridwen spent a moment trying to place which queen she was supposed to be. "After all," she continued, "the theme is past lives. And the poor thing has been re-potted enough times to qualify, I'm sure."

"Re-potted?" Mrs. Gray was eyeing the oleander with mistrust since it was responsible for upsetting her careful decorating.

"Yes. I'm not surprised you don't recognize it. It used to be much smaller. It's the oleander that used to sit on Mary's desk in the estate office. It's done quite well for itself over the years, don't you think?" Joan smiled in the vague way she had and swanned on past them, clearly certain of getting her way.

"As long as it's out of the traffic flow, I really don't care." Mrs. Gray swept off towards the kitchen, capitulating with bad grace. And with her went another missed opportunity to ask her any questions. The only time that Jane was going to allow Cerridwen to ask someone questions, and the woman would not be still.

Teddy's dry chuckle caught her attention. "She's used to getting her own way, is Lilith. Even with her father, who was rumored to have a will of iron. They fight they had over her wedding was legendary." He shook his head over the remembered ruckus.

"Had strong opinions about flower arrangements, did he?" Cerridwen asked as they moved down the hall towards the ballroom, skirting the large house plant which no one had bothered to shift.

"Oh no, her father couldn't care less about flowers." Teddy offered his arm. "He had strong opinions about race and employment. And Toad, as he was often called, was of mixed race and in trade to boot. A hard pill for Daddy to swallow. But it all worked out in the end."

"So they learned to like each other?"

"God no!" Teddy had to come to a stop he was laughing so hard. "They learned they needed each other. But each would still have cheerfully knifed the other given the chance. The old man had made one or two financial missteps, you see. Set to lose everything. And Toad had a gift for numbers. He saved the family holdings from the auction block. And Lilith's old man opened doors that would have otherwise have been closed to someone of mixed race and lower than middle class. Made pots of money together, as I recall."

"Mr. Gray was mixed race?" Cerridwen had a hard time picturing this. Perhaps it had been another form of not-so teenage rebellion. "Lucky for Mrs. Gray that they found some common ground. It isn't easy living between two strong personalities."

"Mixed race is a relative term. It wasn't his mother being black that was so upsetting to her family as it was his father being French. I wouldn't feel sorry for her if I were you." Teddy turned to look toward the entry where rising voices could be heard once again. "Like I said, she has always gotten her way in one way or another."

They came to a stop in the huge double doors leading to the ballroom. All the houses in the court, except the Sands' cottage, had a ballroom. Cerridwen had often thought if the Court had had a homeowners association it would have been one of their requirements.

But Whitmore's ballroom was something special. It was quite frankly a nightmare of French Neo-Gothic. Mrs. Gray and Ruby had decided not to fight the décor. It was, after all, a Halloween party. They had used only strategically placed lights to set the mood.

A platform stood at the far end of the ballroom, supporting an impressive array of instruments and equipment. As they moved down the room, Thomas jumped down and headed towards the door. Cerridwen didn't flatter herself that he was coming to greet them. He was obviously on a mission. He didn't even notice them till he was right up on them. He came to a sudden stop.

"Wow," he said, looking Cerridwen up and down. "Just…wow!" He turned to look at Teddy. "And wow. For very different reasons."

"Doesn't Teddy have lovely knees?" Cerridwen couldn't help asking.

"I'm not answering that." Thomas eyed her costume. "Who are you? How does that dress stay on?"

"Louise Brooks, and wouldn't you like to know? Where's your costume?"

He was dressed in black pants and a black sleeveless tee shirt. He reached for something that dangled around his neck and pushed it up over his head. He sprouted antenna from a narrow headband. "I'm an ant. Fred's a snail. I don't know yet if we managed to talk Gerry into being a butterfly."

"You were all insects in a former life?" Teddy asked.

"Well, we thought the Beatles would be a little too obvious. And you can't be reincarnated if you're not dead yet. Fred argued for Keith Richards on the grounds that he was already dead, but we're not sure of a date, and Gerry says you have to die before your next life starts. It was quite the argument."

"Did they resolve it?" The question of reincarnated rockers seemed to hold a fascination for Teddy.

"Not before the beer ran out. I have to go find the breaker box. We've blown something."

“Fuse box,” Cerridwen corrected him. “The electrical hasn’t been updated since 1930.”

“Great, awesome. It gets better and better.” Thomas shook his head and started for the hall. He stopped and came back. Catching Cerridwen unaware, he grabbed her by the shoulders and kissed her. She felt it all the way to her toes. He steadied her for a second. “I really do want to know how that dress is staying on.” She was still trying to catch her breath as he jogged out the door.

“I really don’t think that someone of my tender years should have been forced to witness that kiss.” Teddy studied the ceiling.

“Oh, please.” Cerridwen tried to repair the damage to her hair. “You have not only seen worse, you’ve done worse.”

“Yes.” Teddy smiled happily. “Yes, I have.”

The fuses were restored. The caterers finished setting up without incident. The party started with a bang. The band opened with a metal version of “Night on Bald Mountain,” which was very well received by everyone but Mrs. Gray. Ruby, of course, thought it was fabulous.

Ruby had come as Mati Hari. The effect was stunning. Pearl was dressed as Mary Shelly. She spent a lot of time telling people this. Felix came as Lord Byron and spent a heated ten minutes explaining to a Cleopatra that “No, he was not a vampire. Vampires were not historical figures. They were both imaginary and immortal, making reincarnation an impossibility on a number of counts.” It went downhill from there when Cleo assumed number of counts was a play on words.

As the night progressed, Mrs. Gray’s lips got tighter and tighter. The band swung from a guitar heavy version of “Monster Mash,” made just a little creepy by Thomas’s deep voice, to a very metal cover of “Tainted Love.” Mrs. Gray’s expression became strained as she eyed Ruby across the room. Apparently Ruby had not seen fit to tell her what kind of band she had managed to line up at the last minute. This was one situation where Lilith had not gotten her way.

Joan was enjoying herself. Now and then she looked almost like the woman Cerridwen remembered. Before the disturbed child began to emerge, her behavior was erratic, but considering the events of the last month, perhaps it was to be expected.

Thorn had been released on probation after admitting to the break-in. It had made social interactions awkward, to say the least. Mrs. Gray and Thorn seemed to be avoiding each other. Or rather, Mrs. Gray was avoiding Thorn and he was making no effort to pursue her. It wasn't obvious at first. She had plenty to keep her busy. But as the night went on, she made sure that these tasks took her where he wasn't. They had been part of Witt's weird little family at the same time. Shouldn't they have some common interests, at least some common memories? Yet Mrs. Gray was making a concentrated effort to ignore Thorn.

"I would have thought you two would have a lot to talk about." Cerridwen gestured with her glass to where Mrs. Gray was riding herd on a caterer that didn't really need it.

"I don't see why. We didn't have anything to say to each other back in the day. Why should now be any different?" Thorn shrugged. Having got his outburst out of his system in Cerridwen's office, he was back to his old monosyllabic self.

"You lived in the same house and didn't talk to each other?" Cerridwen told herself that she was not sticking her nose in, she was just making conversation.

"She had no use for me. And I had less for her. She modeled for me a few times. But once she realized I wasn't looking for a muse to obsess over, she lost interest. For all her topless ramblings, she was always a snob. Why she fixed on Toad of all people, I'll never know. I would have thought a glorified accountant was beneath her." He dismissed the subject with a tilt of his nearly empty glass. Cerridwen was silent for a moment as she tried to clear her mind of a topless Mrs. Gray.

"Maybe she saw something others didn't. It's difficult to know what goes on inside a relationship from the outside. I think it was Ann Landers who said 'only the two people inside a marriage know what's truly going on. And one of them is wrong.' And you never can tell what will attract someone." Cerridwen scanned the crowd. Joan's parties were always a great place to people watch.

"She admires people who are good with money," was Thorn's tart reply. This was a side of Thorn she had seen at her house the other day, bitter and talkative. "And I hear Toad pulled her father's ass out of the financial fire. Although how he did that without a ton of cash up front, I never figured out."

"How much cash, in your opinion?" An idea was forming.

"I don't know. Twenty, maybe thirty thousand." He shrugged.

"What if he got it from more than one source, like a little bit here and there?"

Thorn turned a suddenly intense stare on her. "You could if you skimmed it from multiple sources?" He might have said more, but his attention was claimed by a young woman dressed as Julia Margaret Cameron, who was the only person to recognize his costume as Joseph Nicephore Niepce, inventor of the camera obscura.

"Of course," she said to herself. "A sane person simply would leave it alone."

"Talking to yourself?" Thorn asked. Julia Margaret Cameron had wandered off.

"Sometimes it's the only guarantee of intelligent conversation," Cerridwen answered absently.

"Toad kept the books before Mary came." He didn't wait for a reply. "If someone was skimming, it had to be him. That must be what she was worried about before she disappeared." He set his glass down with a thump. "It would explain where Toad got the cash to save Lilith's family."

It had finally pierced Thorn's ego that whatever had gone on that long ago summer, not all of it had been about him. It had only taken him fifty years. Cerridwen could see him finally wondering if it could it be a reason to kill Mary Paul. "Toad never struck me as capable of murder, though. Didn't like to get his hands dirty. I need another drink." He picked up his glass and took off, cutting through the scattered dancers. He hadn't waited for a reply.

It was just as well. Cerridwen didn't have one.

Up on the stage, the boys tore into "Sweet Dreams" by the Eurthymics. Through the mob of dancers Cerridwen could see Michael Stone propped against a gratuitous pillar. She caught his eye and he waded through the crowd toward her.

"You're not avoiding me?" he asked with inebriated cheerfulness.

"There seems to be an awful lot of avoiding going on tonight. And there seems to be little reason for it," she answered.

"It's got around that I'm Mary's nephew. Everybody is wondering if that revenge theory you put forward had some truth to it. They think I tried to poison Joan and freeze dried the Hawkner."

"It was a joke. I wasn't even aware you were related when I tossed it off," Cerridwen objected.

"You think that holds any water? They're all keeping their distance while they try to decide if I killed Ann Hawkner. Do you think I offed her?"

"That takes Hawkner's involvement in Mary's murder as a foregone conclusion."

Stone waved this off. "But you thought it, at least for a minute, didn't you? I didn't understand why you were so nervous this morning. You thought I was threatening you." Before she could speak, he continued, "I wasn't, you know. I was trying to figure out what I had done to give myself away. And then it turns out that I had simply overestimated my own importance." He gave her a self-deprecating smile.

He had never known his aunt. How real was Mary to him? Would he be so enamored of his aunt's disappearance if it wasn't so obviously bestseller material? Cerridwen tried to decide if he cared enough about a distant ideal to kill. She didn't like the man and wanted to believe that he would. It might feel that way to her because Stone had scared the crap out of her earlier. She thought changing the subject was her safest option.

"What I would like to know is how everybody and his brother knew I was having my locks changed."

"I didn't know it was supposed to be a secret." She had caught Stone's attention at last.

"You knew as well? Who felt the need to tell everyone this?" Cerridwen gave a thought to an alarm system as well as new locks.

"Joan mentioned it. A while ago. Not sure when. It was after the cops brought her that earring. Something about a key gone missing. Felix and I talked about it. And I'm fairly sure I mentioned it to Hawkner. It got her all excited for some reason. Said she would have to tell her little history friends at the next meeting." Stone summarily dismissed the Victoria Historical Society.

Cerridwen was fairly sure that was not the phrasing that Hawkner had used. Before she could pry anything else interesting out of him, Stone wandered off.

Bits of information, none connecting to the other, floated about inside her head. The whole situation was giving her a headache. Once again she reflected on how badly plotted life was.

The band took a break and she was amused to note that they had talked Gerry into the butterfly wings after all. They were tired, their clothes damp with sweat.

"Are you done for the night?" Cerridwen asked.

"No. We have another hour to go. Twenty minute break. Catch our breath." Fred answered in gasps. Thomas was busy downing water. Gerry looked at his bottle and then simply poured it over himself. A few dribbles clung to his wings. Cerridwen watched them trickle to the floor as she thought out loud, "I can't narrow it down by who had knowledge of my locks. And I still don't know who the second intruder was."

"I thought that was Thorn" Fred was still breathless.

"No." Gerry pushed wet hair out of his eyes. "Cerridwen means the second intruder from the first break-in. Not the intruder from the second break-in."

"You only have Joan's word for it that there was one," Fred pointed out from his spot on the floor. He couldn't quite lie down. The large twist of fabric that served as his snail shell was in the way.

Cerridwen considered this for a moment. "No," Cerridwen said. "There was someone there, I think. I don't know, it's just a feeling. But Joan doesn't lie. Even if she is off her rocker. She'll bend and twist the truth like a pipe cleaner, but she won't outright lie. When I asked her about the keys, she practically vibrated with the effort."

"Maybe it's been two people all along and the two murders are unrelated," Gerry said.

"They're too similar to be two different people." Thomas voice was muffled because he still sat doubled up with his head in his hands. Ruby made hurry-up gestures from near the stage. The three of them went back to work, taking nearly all the bottled water with them. Their take on "This is Halloween" from *The Nightmare Before Christmas* followed her to the bar.

"Would you look at this? This knife is filthy." Mrs. Gray lifted a sharp and shiny chief's knife from the buffet table. Cerridwen turned to answer her, but she swept by in pursuit of the caterers, a wave of carnation-scented perfume wafting in her wake. Thorn made to intercept her. Gray sidestepped neatly calling to Joan as she headed out into the hall.

Cerridwen watched Thorn weave through the crowd. She thought about what Thomas had said. There was a certain sameness about the murders. Not quite a bid for attention—more like the attention was a foregone conclusion. Someone used to the spotlight, maybe. Though there was an element of spite to Hawkner's death, as well. The scarf had been an extra, and unnecessary, slap. She let go of the thought. It wasn't working. Time to try a different approach.

Cerridwen headed for Ruby with a growing feeling of dread. The problem was, she'd forced herself to think about this whole thing like real life. Time to give that up and look at it like a book. In a book it was always the least likely person. I took her almost ten minutes to chase down Ruby.

"Where's Joan?" Cerridwen asked when she finally ran Mati Hari to ground.

"I don't know," Ruby answered. "Joan said something about trimming the oleander. Of all the times to think of gardening! And now I can't find her or Mrs. Gray."

That was when the old house decided it had had enough. The fuses gave out all at once. The lights went out.

Chapter 28

Cerridwen abandoned Ruby and ran out into the hallway. She admitted to herself that that was a very stupid thing to do, as she crashed into someone in the dark. Wasn't she always saying nasty things about authors who had their heroines rushing off alone into God knows what?

After a moment it was clear that she had collided with two bodies. She, Fred, and Teddy took a while to untangle themselves. It took longer because Teddy's armor kept snagging on things.

"Where's Mrs. Gray?" Cerridwen thrust Teddy away from her.

"She was in the entry with Joan a moment ago. I think they were headed to the sun room," Teddy answered, buffing his breast plate.

"Did she have a knife?" Cerridwen knew the question was melodramatic but couldn't tamp down the growing dread.

"Yes, as a matter a fact. Thought that a bit odd." Teddy frowned.

The sounds of a scuffle echoed in the entry. Cerridwen made a decision. She really hoped it wasn't a stupid one.

"Teddy, go find Jane. And have someone get the lights back on. Fred, come with me. We need to find Joan and Mrs. Gray right now." Without waiting for an answer, she grabbed Fred and hauled him down the hall toward the sun room.

"What is going on?" Fred was his usual unruffled self.

"Mrs. Gray's husband was skimming money from Witt. I'm pretty sure that's how he pulled her father's business out of its tailspin."

"And?" Fred felt she should elaborate.

"That's about as far as I got before I realized Mrs. Gray is wandering the darkened halls with a knife." Cerridwen felt her way down the hall.

"Fair enough." Fred followed her into the dark.

Thomas took an indirect route through the darkened ballroom, avoiding the mass of confused humanity on the dance floor. Near the bar he got caught in Gerry's wings. He grabbed a fist full of gossamer and dragged him along, too. In the hall the wings snagged on Teddy's armor as they were blinded by his flashlight.

"What the fuck is going on?" Thomas wrenched the two apart.

"Fuses. Cerridwen said get the lights on. Went after Mrs. Gray with a knife. Stopped to find a flashlight." Teddy picked shreds of gauze out of his chainmail. Thomas sorted this out.

"Who had the knife?"

"Mrs. Gray. But it's all right. Cerridwen has Fred."

"Right. Gerry, lights. Teddy, with me."

"Wait." The older man pulled him to a halt. "I have the light." They looked at the Maglite and then down the hall towards the front of the house. "On second thought, you go first. You're scarier." Teddy pushed him forward. The erratic beam bounced off the walls and skittered across the floor, catching on something near the stairs.

Thomas reached behind him and took the light, training it on the dark shape. Thorn's frock coat was ripped and crumpled, but the real damage was to his head. The blow had crushed the side of his skull. The puddle under him was not just blood.

Thomas felt sick. Mary Paul's bones had been surreal. Hawkner was a Popsicle. This was disturbing on a whole new Technicolor level.

Teddy knelt at the edge of light.

"What are you doing?"

"Checking for signs of life." There was an unsettling confidence in his motions.

"How do you even know how to do that?"

"You would be amazed at some of the things I picked up along the way. Unfortunately, raising the dead isn't one of them. There isn't anything we can do for him." Teddy stood and wiped his hands on the hem of his tunic.

"Are you sure? Maybe CPR…"

"Thomas, his brain is in pieces on the floor, along with the majority of his blood. Take the light, find Cerridwen. I'm going to get Jane. We need to find Mrs. Gray. If she's panicked to the point that she smashed Thorn's skull, I don't think much of Joan's, or Cerridwen's, chances."

"You think Mrs. Gray did this?" Thomas was doubtful.

"Well, I doubt it was Joan, and Gray was the one with the knife," Teddy said with a shrug.

"My money's on Cerridwen."

"She's not the one with the knife," Teddy reminded him.

* * * *

One wrong turn and a broom closet later, Cerridwen and Fred came to the door of the sun room. The lights were out here, too, but there was a moon and enough light filtered through the glass and out into the hall for them to see what was happening. The carnation scent of Mrs. Gray's perfume lingered in the hall. Cerridwen thought it must have been that and not the crushed flowers she had smelled the night of the first break-in. That was why the scent was so strong. Mrs. Gray had to have been the second intruder.

"What did you do with my father's journal?" Joan's voice echoed off the wall of glass.

"Is that what this is about? Is that why you're trying to ruin my life?" Mrs. Gray bounced from frantic to incredulous. Her famous calm had completely evaporated. "You thought I hid it somewhere? I destroyed it years ago. You think I would have left it lying around? The idiot wrote everything down!" She shoved Joan into a chair. Cerridwen and Fred crept through the door.

"What was there to write down?" Joan tried to sit up, then flinched away from Gray's waving knife.

"His vision of Mary ascending to heaven was a blow by blow account of Todd and me hiding Mary. He must have been higher than a kite when he saw us. But it was all there. I burned the thing."

"Who is Todd?" Joan was confused.

"Toad!" screamed Mrs. Gray. Cerridwen and Joan both flinched.

"Then why were you in Cerridwen's house, if you weren't looking for that journal?"

Cerridwen paused at the sound of her name and then continued inching toward Joan as Fred edged along the wall, trying to get behind Mrs. Gray.

"For the stupid account book. I knew Mary had hidden it somewhere. The only place left was that damn table. And then your idiot of a Father sold it to that Frey woman. And she would never let me in the house, like I was some kind of stalker or tabloid reporter. Jumped up daughter of theater people. I thought it would be easier once she was dead. I waited years. But she left it to her granddaughter instead of the city or the Historical Society like a decent, civic-minded person. And that twit ignored all my attempts to get in the place. She was always busy. Writing all the time. Like what she does is work." Mrs. Gray's disdain was palpable.

Fred moved forward another inch. The door to the service corridor cracked open. Thomas eased into the room doing an admirable imitation of an eel for a man his size.

"Why are you explaining all of this to me? You think I won't tell anyone?" Joan demanded.

Cerridwen swore under her breath. They wanted Gray to keep talking, at least until Jane got here. Gray had hold of the knife again. If she stopped talking, she might start stabbing. And nobody wanted that.

"You're not going to tell anybody anything. You're going to make another suicide attempt. And this time you're going to be successful. You killed Mary and then you killed Hawkner and Thorn to cover it up. You couldn't handle the guilt anymore. "

"You don't know Thorn is dead." Joan's voice quavered.

"Please. You heard the noise his head made when it struck the newel post. You really think anyone could survive that crunch?"

Joan shuddered.

Mrs. Gray blandished the knife. "I put more sleeping pills in your drink. Soon you'll start to lose consciousness. Then all that's left to do is slit your wrists and let you bleed out on the floor. Messy, but can't be helped. Needs must. At least it's suitably dramatic."

Amateur, fumed Cerridwen. Didn't she realize that they would be able to tell someone else had made the cuts? Didn't anybody do any research? This was the information age. There was no excuse. Never mind that the dimwit had not even considered how many doors there were to this room.

"But I didn't drink it," Joan said.

Both Cerridwen and Mrs. Gray froze.

"What?" said Gray

"I didn't drink the glass with the pills in it. I remember what you did to Mary. I have for some time, Lilith. I know that you poisoned her with the leaves from the oleander in her office. The same plant that stands next to the stairs right now. I would have put the same in your drink. But something more fitting occurred to me."

"What are you talking about? What have you done!" The hysteria was winning. Years of pent-up fear were taking their toll.

"Blind as a bat. Mad as a hatter," Joan said.

"Are you calling me crazy? You should talk. Your father thought you were nuts. I had him convinced you killed Mary. Did you know that? Poor Joan and her Electra complex. What was a father to do but cover it up?"

"Dry as a bone. The bowl and the bladder lose their tone," Joan went on in a sing-song tone.

"You're spouting nonsense. You're playing for time. It won't help." Mrs. Gray had regained some of her composure.

But Joan had never lost hers, Cerridwen was beginning to understand.

"And the heart runs alone. Only a matter of time now." With timing worthy of a B movie, the lights came on. At the same time the figurative light went on for Mrs. Gray.

"Jimsonweed! You poisoned me with that damn tea!"

All three women stood still for a moment staring at each other. Thomas was flat against the opposite wall. Fred was crouched against the wall behind Mrs. Gray. Neither of them would be able to reach her in time. She took one look at Cerridwen, clearly visible with the lights on, and charged at Joan with the knife raised. Cerridwen moved between them, throwing her arms around Joan.

There was a rush of air and crash of glass. Cerridwen waited for the knife to fall but it never came.

Thomas made a rush at Gray at the same time Jane and Jesús kicked open the outer door. Thomas, who was closer, reached Gray first, with Fred not far behind, and wrapped his arms around her and lifted her off the floor. She screamed and struggled, slashing and stabbing with the knife. He grunted and swore.

Jesús and Fred moved to help him. She slashed at them as well, screaming words so colorful that Cerridwen was surprised she knew them. Jane grabbed Gray's wrist and yanked backward. There was an audible pop and snap and with a cry, Gray dropped the knife. She went limp and Thomas and Jesús had to scramble to catch her.

"Really, boys?" Jane kicked the knife aside. "It takes three of you? And you didn't even disarm her." She shook her head in disappointment. Jane began to read Mrs. Gray her rights. She pulled out her handcuffs, fastening them in front in deference to Gray's dislocated wrist.

"I need a doctor. That Witt woman has poisoned me. She admitted it! Let me go."

As Teddy had said, she was used to getting her own way. It didn't seem to occur to her that today should be any different. The two detectives simply ignored the outburst.

"No, she didn't," Cerridwen said, still holding a trembling Joan. "Well, I mean Joan did tell you that, but she didn't actually poison you. At least not with jimsonweed. You'd be hallucinating by now if you weren't dead. It takes effect relatively quickly. You should remember that, Lilith."

Jane shushed Cerridwen with a look. "Well, *I* would have remembered." Cerridwen mumbled under her breath defiantly.

Felix chose that moment to sweep in and take in the situation with one glance. He stepped to one side as they escorted Mrs. Gray out through a curious crowd. He unwound his cravat and began to fold it as he advanced on Thomas. "You're bleeding everywhere. I trust someone thought to call an ambulance?"

Everyone turned to look at Thomas. There were shallow cuts all up and down his arms. Three gashes in the front of his shirt were sluggishly bleeding.

"Doesn't that hurt?" Fred wanted to know. "'Cause the ones on my arm sting like a son of a bitch."

"Well, now that I've noticed it, it hurts like hell." Thomas pulled the fabric this way and that, trying to get a better look at the cuts. He was hampered by Felix, who was trying to bandage him with the cravat.

"It's the adrenaline," Jane told him. "When it wears off, you will feel everything."

Gerry charged through the crowd in the door. "Hey, guys. I got the lights back on."

Chapter 29

Blue Scrubs was horrified to see them again. For a moment, Cerridwen was sure that he was going to break and run. But he pulled himself together and cleaned and bandaged Fred and Thomas. The stab wounds on Thomas's chest required stitches, and he hummed happily as the mild painkiller took effect.

They had arrived at the hospital with appropriate fanfare, sirens blaring. Lilith Gray was down the hall alternating silence and fury while her wrist was treated. For a wonder Blue Scrubs seemed more afraid of her than Cerridwen, although it was a bit of a tossup.

"The medication shouldn't affect you this way." Blue Scrubs frowned at Thomas who had progressed from humming to singing something melodic in Russian. His voice matched his size and it traveled easily through the entire unit. "I didn't give you that large a dose."

"There is a chance it is interacting with the vodka," Thomas allowed mid-verse.

"How much did you have?" Blue Scrubs asked sharply.

"One."

"One drink?"

"No. One bottle."

"Mixed with what?" Blue Scrubs wanted to know.

Thomas blinked at him. "You're supposed to mix it?" It seemed a foreign concept.

Blue Scrubs gave a sigh but finished his task without another word. When Jane arrived to collect them, he greeted her with something akin to joy, muttering something that sounded like "And good luck," under his breath he left the room.

"I'm sorry I thought you were Mary's long lost murderous relative," Cerridwen said as Blue Scrubs made good his escape. From his expression she was sure he heard her, but he did not reply.

Jane herded them back to Witt's End and cornered them in the grand salon with ruthless efficiency. None of them had the strength to resist. By then it was nearly dawn. The Sand sisters were lying in wait with tea and gin. Felix was just lying in wait. It was hard to tell if Stone was there on purpose or had just been sucked along by sheer force of personality.

"I suppose you have the whole thing figured out and are ready to explain it to me." There was an edge to Jane's statement that would not allow it to be a question.

"Not all of it," Cerridwen qualified. She sat down on the other side of Thomas who, she told herself, she was not using as a shield. Although she had little choice. He had refused to let go of her since the sun room. It had made treating him an interesting exercise for Blue Scrubs. "I had thought that Toad had killed Mary and Mrs. Gray was just covering for him. But Mrs. Gray says she killed Mary Paul. I'm fairly sure that it was because Mary had worked out that Toad was embezzling."

"She killed to cover for him? That's true love right there." Fred shifted to make room for Jesús on the love seat.

"I think it's more that Lilith loved herself enough to kill. Her father was facing financial ruin. That would have had a serious impact on her chosen lifestyle. Toad had enough socked away to solve all her problems and support her in a way she was more than accustomed to. But if Toad were caught, all that lovely money went away."

"But then nothing for five decades. And Toad is dead now," Fred said. Thomas had begun to sing again. Fred kicked him and he stopped. He explained to Cerridwen, "You have to hit Thomas' reset button every so often."

"Gray had been trying to get the account book for some time. Toad didn't tell her about it till just before his death...last year? It took her awhile to work out where it was. That was why she broke into Joan's house last year. She hadn't realized that Witt had sold the table. And then she had had no luck getting in Cerridwen's house. Cerridwen's grandmother didn't like Mrs. Gray. When Gray broke in Cerridwen's and ran into Joan, she figured Joan must have remembered what had happened," Jane explained.

"Gray didn't know where in the house the table was and she cut her losses when Joan showed up," Cerridwen added.

"Gray had managed to confuse the issue so much at the time that no one was sure what, if anything, had happened to Mary. But once Mary was found, the whole thing began to come apart," Jane said. "Witt had known something bad had happened to Mary, but he believed that Toad was behind it. He couldn't prove anything though. The jimsonweed he took on a regular basis made the whole episode a muddle in his head. And Gray had worked so hard to implicate Joan he couldn't be sure. He wrote everything down in the journal that Joan was looking for."

"Mrs. Gray had stolen and destroyed the journal shortly after Mary's murder. She convinced Witt that no one would believe Joan wasn't involved and that the best way to protect her was to keep the whole thing quiet."

"What I don't understand is why Gray left the body in the tree," Thomas said. "That skeleton scared the piss out me."

"It was an easy hiding place at the time. And certainly no one thought to look there. She probably meant to move it later. But you remember Mr. Demetriov said there had been a storm not long after, and the block and tackle that had been used to build the fountain fell and was never replaced. Gray decided to leave well enough alone. I wouldn't be surprised if, in the long run, she had simply pushed the whole thing out of her mind," Cerridwen said.

Both detectives turned hard stares on Cerridwen.

"No," Jane said. "We don't remember Mr. Demetriov saying that."

"Oh well, maybe you weren't there. I thought I had mentioned it to you." Cerridwen had the grace to be chagrined.

"So it was Gray that sold Joan that story about the spirit in the tree?" Fred kicked Thomas again who simply kicked him back this time.

"No," Joan said as she slipped in the door without any of them noticing. There was a flurry of movement as both Jesús and Fred tried to give her their seat. "Funnily enough, it was Mary that told me that story. She saw me climbing it one day. She was afraid that I would hurt myself. The week before she disappeared, Thorn and I were in the tree. And Thorn fell. That's how he got that awful scar on his wrist. Mary was furious with him, and she was scared I would get hurt next time. The fairy tale was a bribe to stay on the ground. I clung to it after she disappeared, perhaps longer than I should have."

"So all was well until a Nerf football ruined everything," Thomas told the ceiling. He rubbed at his chest. The painkiller was wearing off.

"Even then, Gray might have been all right if she hadn't done for Hawkner," was Gerry's opinion.

"But something had to be done about Hawkner," Jane told him. "She had always been an irritant, but lately she had become a danger. She was old enough to remember the events of that August with some clarity and she knew about Gray's need to get in the house. When she told Gray about Cerridwen changing the locks, there was a 'tantrum of epic proportions,' according to members of the Historical Society. It was enough out of character that, along with a few other things, Hawker began to suspect what had really happened."

"Was she trying to blackmail Mrs. Gray?" Cerridwen could easily believe it of her.

"No." Jesús shook his head. "That's what I suspected at first as well. But Ms. Hawkner had more moral fiber than anyone suspected. She had idealized Mrs. Gray to the point of imitation. I think it was painful for her when she realized that her idol had feet of clay. She had every intention of telling us what she knew. But she thought it a courtesy to tell Mrs. Gray what she meant to do. She might have hoped that her idol would turn herself in."

"Mrs. Gray may even have told the Hawkner that she was going to do just that. It would have taken the sleeping pills time to take effect. Who knows what they talked about?" Cerridwen was lost for a moment in the possibilities.

Joan stirred, reminding Cerridwen that this was not her imaginary world where she could rearrange and even resurrect people at will.

"That's why Mrs. Gray tried to drug me. She meant to get rid of me and frame me for Ann's murder all at once." Joan laughed. It shook in the middle and tried to turn into tears instead. "It must have been so frustrating for her when I didn't die."

Jason, who had followed his mother in and sat quietly up to now, put his arm around her. She leaned on him.

"It must have been a bit of a shock. Mrs. Gray had made such careful plans. I think she even said it herself to us at one point. Lilith really was genuinely used to getting her way—all her life," Cerridwen said.

"And when I waved that oleander under her nose, she knew for certain that I remembered that afternoon. She decided I had to go. I couldn't be allowed to ruin her life anymore." Joan clutched her hands together in an effort to stop them from shaking.

Cerridwen wondered at her composure under the stress she had endured.

"You saw her kill Mary?" Ruby slipped in on the other side of Joan, annexing the love seat in one move. Fred and Jesús stood uncertainly to one side.

"I didn't understand at the time. I saw Lilith make the tea, but the leaves were the wrong shape. It made Mary sick. Almost everyone was out that day. When they came back, Lilith told them Mary had left.

It wasn't till later that I worked out where the leaves had come from and exactly what Lilith had done. I wanted to believe I was wrong. And I had no proof."

"But why did she kill Thorn?" Fred's expression tightened. Cerridwen thought he must be recalling the mangled body. They had had to pass it on the way out of Whitmore and they had all had a good view. Jesús had been right. Thorn had resembled a pile of discarded laundry.

"That was my fault." Cerridwen felt sick at the idea. "I was thinking out loud. I may have said that if Toad was keeping the books, he must have been the one skimming money from Witt. I honestly don't remember if that part was out load. Thorn must have heard me musing. Whatever I said was the last piece Thorn needed. He suspected Mrs. Gray. But he wasn't sure why she had done it. People always want to know why. He confronted her. She saw it as solving a problem. She would 'discover' Joan's body, plant the idea that Joan had killed Thorn before committing suicide."

"She claims it was an accident. She says he rushed her with the knife and she had to defend herself," Jane said.

"No." Joan shook her head. "He rushed at us, but she had the knife. He jumped back when he saw it. And then she shoved him. He fell against the newel post. But if that hadn't happened, I'm sure she would have thought of something."

"You have to admire her ability to think on her feet," Cerridwen said with grudging respect.

"No, you really don't," Jane answered. "People are dead. She killed them. We've been up all night trying to clear this up. I had to take statements from a ballroom full of people, process a crime scene, and I still have an unbelievable amount of paperwork ahead of me. I don't admire her at all."

"Look on the bright side. With Mrs. Gray under arrest, the Historical Society will probably be too embarrassed to give anyone any trouble about anything," Fred said.

"Oh, well, isn't that a comfort." Jane's tone made it clear it wasn't.

"Lilith couldn't have done everything alone. Toad had to help her with the body. Even with the aid of the block and tackle, she had to have help." Ruby continued to pat a shaking Joan. "What? I can't be the only one to think it. Thomas, you've been up that tree. Think of the coordination it would have taken to hang on to the rope and shove her in the hole. Sorry, dear." This last was in response to a whimper of protest from Joan.

"I can't work out how you would do it with only one person, either," Jesús admitted to professional curiosity.

"She got Toad to help her." Felix maintained an air of elegance even without the cravat. "Either from love, or fear. She had a hold over him if she knew where the money had come from. On the other hand, she had just killed to cover for him."

"He couldn't have helped with Hawkner, though. He's been dead for more than a year," Jesús said. "How does a woman in her seventies haul all that dead weight?"

"That Gray could have managed...the snow was icy and slick. Maybe she slid the body," was Jane's opinion. "It's a matter of leverage. And it's not as if she was in any hurry. It had started to snow in earnest by then. The city was all but at a standstill. With everybody holed up, there was very little chance of being seen."

"It would have been easier to leave Hawkner where she fell. And easier to make it look like an accidental overdose. No one thought for a minute that she had dragged herself out there and built the snowman." Gerry had shed his wings before driving to the hospital. He looked a little forlorn without them.

"It wasn't that bad of an idea." Felix hitched his trousers and crossed his legs. "It confused the time of death, which is always useful, as I'm sure Cerridwen can tell you."

"You really think she put that much thought into it? I would say it was more from anger than reason." Cerridwen chewed her lip.

"Maybe she didn't plan on the snow melting so quickly. We all think badly of the others not noticing Mary was gone. But how soon would any of us have looked for Hawkner?" Stone said. "I for one would have just enjoyed the silence."

The truth of that observation made more than one of them shift uncomfortably.

"But why the graffiti? I did it because I was a scared kid. But she was trying to hide something. Why call attention to it?" Joan was calmer now, but the strain still showed. The strain of the last month would tell on all of them. And it had been a much longer ordeal for Joan, lasting the better part of her life. Jason hugged his mother.

"That was me, actually." Stone's answer was sheepish. "I wanted to stir things up. See who reacted. I should have thought about the distress it would cause you. But I didn't know where to start, and I was fishing for anything."

Jason glared daggers at him. If Cerridwen was Stone, she wouldn't go anywhere alone with Jason. But chances were Jane would have some things to say to him on the topic as well.

Jane and Jesús had to go back to work. They had a long night ahead of them.

As he stepped over Gerry's feet, Jesús stopped and stared. He looked from Gerry to Fred and back. "Fred and Ginger! Fred Astaire and Ginger Rogers. Oh, my God, I just got that."

"Why else did you think we were calling him Ginger?" Fred asked.

"Because he has red hair?" said Jesús, chagrined.

"Well, look at it this way. At least you're pretty." Gerry patted Jesús on the shoulder. The others lingered, trying to make sense of the events of the last month. The morning light was turning the windows from gray to gold before people started to drift home. Eventually only Thomas and his roommates were left.

"Come on, Teddy. It's past your bed time." Gerry pushed him towards the door.

"Shows what you know. You young people, no stamina." Teddy pouted while Fred stifled a yawn.

Thomas dragged himself to his feet. "I guess I should take another painkiller and go to bed," he said mournfully.

Cerridwen paused in the door to the hall. "Fred, do me a favor and lock the door on your way out. Thomas, turn off the lights before you come upstairs."

It took Thomas longer than it should have to work out what she meant. Maybe it was the painkillers. But to his credit, once he got it, he beat her up the stairs. They could hear Fred shushing Teddy's laughter as they shut the door.

The End

Made in the USA
Middletown, DE
07 August 2020

14651578R00126